THE HOT SPOT

NIOBIA
BRYANT

Ke... rp.

DAFINA BOOKS are published by

Kensington Publishing Corp.
119 West 40th Street
New York, NY 10018

All Kensington Titles, Imprints, and Distributed Lines are available at special quantity discounts for bulk purchases for sales promotions, premiums, fund-raising, and educational or institutional use. Special book excerpts or customized printings can also be created to fit specific needs. For details, write or phone the office of the Kensington special sales manager: Kensington Publishing Corp., 119 West 40th Street, New York, NY 10018, attn: Special Sales Department, Phone: 1-800-221-2647.

ISBN-13: 978-0-7582-6535-7
ISBN-10: 0-7582-6535-2

First mass market printing: August 2011

10 9 8 7 6 5 4 3 2 1

Printed in the United States of America

THE HOT SPOT

Kaleb lifted Zaria's body up against his, before turning to press her back against the front door of her home. As he brought his hands down to cup her full buttocks, he brought his face in close to hers.

Zaria tightened her hold around his neck, feeling secure in his embrace as her eyes flitted over his face as if memorizing every detail. She tilted her chin up to trace the full outline of his mouth with the tip of her tongue, enjoying the way her body trembled. She laughed huskily as he pressed his mouth to the corner of hers. "Things are going so fast," she whispered against his lips.

Kaleb leaned back to look down at her, liking how the porch light reflected like twinkling stars in her eyes. "We don't have to do this," he told her. Still he wanted her to *want* this moment.

He eased his hands up under her shirt to press against the warm skin of her waist and stepped back to let her down onto her feet.

She shook her head. "It feels like we have to," she admitted, speaking her feelings. Her body felt alive and vibrant. His touch was like pure energy. His body like the most solid of foundations.

She kissed him again, deepening their connection as she pressed her tongue into his mouth to lightly stroke his own.

"I want you," he moaned against her ear.

Zaria felt completely light-headed and hot and flustered as she took her key from her pocket and unlocked the front door. Stepping away from him, she went inside the house and began to unbutton her shirt. "Come and get me," she said.

Also by Niobia Bryant

Heated
Hot Like Fire
Make You Mine
Give Me Fever
Live and Learn
Show and Tell
Message From a Mistress
Mistress No More
Heat Wave (with Donna Hill and Zuri Day)

Published by Dafina Books

I am a true romantic. I completely believe in
happily-ever-after and destined souls.

I write romance because I believe in romance.

And so this one is
dedicated to my heart.

ACKNOWLEDGMENTS

During the writing of this book, my family suffered a major loss in the unexpected death of my cousin Troy Anthony Blake, whom we all lovingly called "Sire." Words cannot express how deeply I felt his loss, not just because he was blood, but also because he was truly a good person with a good heart and wonderful spirit. He had a smile that was as bright as the sun and had the power to make you smile right along with him. His laughter came from deep within his belly, and it was loud and infectious.

The world needs more men—more people—like our Sire. I know he is an angel in heaven now, but I pray that the Lord blesses us with more kind souls like him here on Earth.

Please rest in peace, Sire.

PROLOGUE

"Hey. This is Ned, Zaria, Meena, and Neema. We're not in. You know what to do. Kisses."

Beep.

"Zaria, this is Hope. And this is Chanci, girl. Girl, you and Ned give that *thang* a break and call us back. Or we'll try your cell. If we don't reach you, we'll see y'all later today. Bye!!!"

Beep.

"Hey, Mama. It's Meena and Neema. We called your cell but it's going straight to voice mail. Call us. We really need a care package. This campus food suuuuuuuucks."

Beep. Beep. Beep.

Using one clear-coated acrylic nail, Zaria Ali hit the button to delete all of the messages. Her childhood best friends, Chanci and Hope, were coming into South Carolina for their annual trip home and had indeed reached her on her cell earlier that day. Her twin daughters finally caught her on her cell to lovingly plead for all the home-baked goodies they wanted shipped overnight.

Zaria sighed heavily. The call she was expecting wasn't on the machine and that hurt. It really hurt.

Not even the thought of her best friends coming for her birthday weekend could make her smile. Chanci was flying in from North Carolina and Hope from Maryland. They had been childhood friends growing up in Summerville, South Carolina. Their lives had taken them in separate directions once they got married and got caught up in their careers. It was Zaria who reached out to them to reconnect after so many years, and the time had faded into nothing as they just fell right in sync with one another. That bond they had formed as children had withstood the years and the hundreds of miles between them.

And she looked forward to their sisterhood, their vibrancy, and the fun they would bring into her life and her world. *Lord knows I need to be cheered up.*

Zaria's eyes shifted around her home. They rested on a hundred different things that would forever hold a memory for her. But it didn't feel like a home anymore. She had thought it was a place meant for happily-ever-after. She was wrong. Painfully so.

No, not tonight. No memories. No regrets.

Her girls would be there, and maybe she'd tell them how Zaria—housewife extraordinaire who made it her business to put her husband before herself—had been made a fool of.

Zaria felt sadness weigh down on her shoulders a bit, but she shook it off. She shook him off. Matter of fact, she was shaking all men off for good. The risk of feeling this kind of hurt again wasn't worth it.

Chanci and Hope would easily take her mind off . . . things. And even if—no, *when*—they gushed about the men and the love in their lives, Zaria would refuse to think of the coulda, woulda, or shoulda with *him.*

No matter how much I miss him.

She'd been his wife since she was eighteen. She grew up in her marriage. She sacrificed so much. Her youth. Her happiness.

As she wiped the tears from her eyes, she wished that she had never gotten married at all. Never believed in love and the happily-ever-after. Never lost herself in the desire to be "the perfect wife."

"From now on, I'm going to enjoy life and never let a man knock at the door of my heart," she promised herself, her voice sounding strange to her own ears in the quiet of the house.

She'd spent the last two weeks singing the lonely-bed-and-brokenhearted blues. Barely been able to get out of bed. Crying until her head hurt and her eyes were sore. Calling his phone and pleading with him to change his mind. Making a complete fool of herself as she fought not to lose her mind. She hadn't told a soul what she was suffering through. Not her friends. Not her kids. No one.

Bzzzzz.

Pushing through the hurt and disappointment, Zaria smiled at the sound of the doorbell as she made her way to the front door. She heard their laughter even through the solid wood. Just knowing they were there to hold her if she faltered, to hug her if she cried, and to tickle her until she laughed made things feel better.

Zaria flung the door open wide, causing a slight draft to shimmy across her legs, bare under the dress she wore. She sadly smiled as Chanci and Hope danced past her into the living room, snapping their fingers and singing an off-key rendition of "Happy Birthday"—the Stevie version.

Shutting the door, Zaria crossed her arms over her chest and listened to their cheerful serenade—a bad one, but a serenade nonetheless.

Chanci closed her beautiful green eyes as she flung her head back and hit a high note that would put a cat's wail to shame.

Hope froze midsentence and looked at Zaria, giving her the mother stare that was all too knowing. "Hold on, Aretha," she said dryly to Chanci, reaching out to lightly grasp her arm to stop her. "What's wrong, Zaria?"

Damn, she's good.

The rest of the song thankfully died from Chanci's lips as she opened her eyes and focused them on Zaria as well. Her face brightened and then became concerned. "Is something wrong?"

That's one thing about good friends. They knew each other—really knew each other—and there wasn't much that could be kept from them. Nothing much at all that could be hidden.

Not happiness. Not joy. Not sadness. Not heartbreak.

And why should it?

Zaria thought of him. All of him. And all of the emotions he brought into her world. The happiness. The joy. The sadness. The heartbreak.

One lone tear raced down her cheek and she swiped it away. Seconds later, their arms were around her, and all at once she felt weak with relief *and* strong from their friendship. In their little huddle, she admitted it. "Ned left me."

Chanci's and Hope's heads lifted. Zaria raised hers as well, and the two women shared a look before forcing their eyes back on her.

Zaria felt a piercing pain radiate across her chest.

"Awwwww," her friends said sympathetically.

Chanci and Hope shared another long look before leading Zaria to the kitchen and pressing her into one of the chairs surrounding the dining table in the breakfast nook.

"This calls for alcohol," Chanci said, her face determined, as if she were preparing for war.

Hope nodded in agreement. "Definitely."

As her friends moved about the kitchen, getting ready for one of their patented gabfests—which always included good food and drink—Zaria knew she would have to tell them about the tragic end to her marriage. She would set aside her embarrassment and bring them into the world of pain caused by the man she had loved and cherished for over twenty years of her life.

And for another woman. A younger woman.

Zaria released a breath shaky with her pain, her shock, and her disappointment. Still she felt some relief because she knew her girls would help her deal with it all.

Thank God for them.

Chapter 1

Two years later

The sound of the music in the club was a mix of a hard-core bass line overlapping a sultry reggae beat. The type of beat to bring out the need for a hard—or soft—body pressed up against someone else. The type of bass to make a heated body tic with each thump. The music made you forget your worries. A lousy day at work. An argument with a lover. The bill collector at the door or the phone ringing off the hook.

Any of it—all of it—was drummed out by the music.

And no one took more advantage of that than Zaria Ali.

She mouthed along with the song—one of her favorites—as she moved her hips like she didn't have a backbone. And even though her eyes were closed and her head was tilted back just a bit, she knew the eyes of men—and a few women—were watching her. Many were trying to build up the nerve to dance with her. A few had tried too bold an approach—a hand on her waist or below it—and were politely brushed aside.

As the live reggae band ended the song, Zaria grooved her way off the small dance floor in her leather booties, making her way to the bathroom as nature called like crazy. Thankfully it was clean and there wasn't a line as long as one of Beyoncé's performance weaves, which was surprising for a Thursday night. In her club adventures, she had seen things that made her afraid to even touch the doorknob and that even made her "perch" over a commode.

After leaving the stall, Zaria made her way to the row of sinks. She flipped her hair over her shoulder as she studied her image and washed her hands. "Not bad at all for forty-two," she said to her reflection, twisting her head this way and that to study herself under the bright lights.

Zaria raked her slender fingers through the twenty inches of her jet-black shiny hair that emphasized her light, creamy complexion and made people assume that she was of mixed heritage, but she wasn't. Her blunt bangs perfectly set off her high cheekbones, pouting mouth, and slanted eyes. She was tall—nearly five ten—but every bit of her size 10 frame was curves, and the skinny jeans she wore emphasized that.

"Humph, to hell with you, Ned," Zaria said, and then instantly hated that thoughts of her ex and her failed marriage still lingered on the edges of everything she did and thought . . . even about herself.

It's just that she couldn't forget all of the emotions she felt because of it. Surprised. Shocked. Lost. Confused. Hurt. Insecure. The list could go on and on.

I should have my shit together by now, right?

It had taken every last second of the last two years to reclaim the confidence a cheating and neglectful husband snatched from her. To see the beauty in the mirror. Most she was born with, but other aspects she'd happily purchased: her hair—it was amazing what five hundred dollars and a hellified weave technician could do for a sistah; her full, lush eyelashes—she swore by MAC; and her two-inch nails—no need to explain.

When she was married to Ned, she had been but a pale version of the woman she saw now. His rules had dictated nothing less. No heavy make-up. No snug clothing. Her real hair in nothing snazzier than a bob. Nothing to draw the eyes of other men.

"If that fool could see me now," Zaria whispered as she twisted and turned a bit in the mirror to see herself from all angles. The twenty pounds she worked hard to drop revealed firm, plump, and high breasts; a relatively flat abdomen; and a perfectly round bottom—her best asset in combination with her curvy hips.

It was the kind of body that defied her age and she knew it. In the tradition of Vivica Fox, Halle Berry, and Salma Hayek, she was fortysomething and fabulous. Forty was the new thirty. She had the kind of body that some twenty-year-old women wished they had and even more twenty-year-old men wished they had in their bed.

Zaria used to think the dumbest thing she ever

did was get married at eighteen years young and think it would last forever. But she topped that single foolish act when she cried like a baby when her high school sweetheart, her husband of twenty-two years and father to her twin daughters, left her two years ago for a twenty-year-old woman.

Viagra addict, she thought sarcastically of her ex.

When she married Ned Ali, he promised her the moon and stars. Too bad in the end he only delivered adultery and heartache. The last few years of their marriage had been pure hell.

Long, lonely nights.

Stilted conversations.

Bitter arguments.

Cold silence.

Robotic sex.

Zaria felt like she had wasted over twenty years of her life trying to be the perfect wife to a less-than-perfect husband. She'd even laid the blame for her unhappiness solely at her own door. *She* was doing something wrong. *She* wasn't sexy enough or supportive enough or anything enough.

In hindsight, she saw the truth of her life. She'd missed out on so much trying to grow up way too fast, far too soon. No dating. No parties. No clubbing. None of the things most teenagers and twentysomethings experienced and learned from. Not even a college education.

Zaria tried to ignore the pang of hurt in her chest. *Lord knows I messed up, and I have plenty of regrets, but no more. . . .*

During the last two years, she had made a concentrated effort to turn her life 180 degrees away from the past. It was entirely different from her happy homemaker days.

Zaria had a new career as a bartender that she loved. Freedom that she cherished. Friends whom she adored. She loved the control of her own life—which meant wearing what she wanted, seeing whom she wanted, and doing whatever she wanted *when* she damn well pleased.

Still, none of it was what she planned the day she got married. Divorce hadn't been a part of the picture at all.

Releasing a heavy breath filled with regrets, she quickly touched up her makeup before heading back to the dance floor, shimmying her feet and hips to the lively sounds of the reggae band that seemed to call to her.

An hour later, Zaria was still in the middle of the crowded dance floor beneath the hot red lights. She danced alone with nothing but the bass-filled music and the body heat pulsating against her frame. She didn't miss the circle of men in T-shirts, button-ups, and jerseys that seemed to be transfixed by her movements. And *that* made her feel like she had the thing she lacked the most in her marriage. Control.

After her divorce, Zaria promised herself she would always be in charge. Life would follow her plan. Everything on her terms. Absolutely everything.

Zaria's eyes opened as she awakened slowly. She released a heavy breath and then frowned at the taste of her own morning breath—made all the more horrible by the liquor residue clinging to her tongue. *Way too much rum punch,* she thought as she slowly sat up in the middle of the bed and held the side of her slightly pounding head.

She winced and then blinked at the scraps of paper littering the top of her lavender silk coverlet. She reached out to drag them all closer, remembering she'd emptied her pockets of them as soon as she walked into her bedroom last night.

A dozen or so numbers pushed into her hand throughout the night. She had to laugh because none of those young hardbodies knew about the finesse of handing a lady his business card—that was, if they even had the kinds of professions that called for them. Oh no, instead, lying between her open legs on the bed were bits and pieces of paper, napkins, gum wrappers, the torn corner of a club flyer, and even a receipt. All with the names and numbers of men who wanted to get to know her better.

But nothing about the men stood out to her, and she knew she would never call them as she scooped up all the confetti and leaned over to drop them into the top drawer of her nightstand atop the rest of her "souvenirs." As if it wasn't full enough.

The drawer was her trophy, her misplaced self-esteem during the first year after her divorce. *Who gives a damn if Ned didn't want me? I have the names and numbers of plenty of men who do. Men to be called at my whim—well, if I had planned on calling them.*

Climbing from the bed, she stretched her limbs in her blue lace bikini and matching tank before using her knee to close the drawer. Her stomach grumbled loudly, but she stopped to brush her teeth and wash last night's makeup from her face before finally leaving her bedroom on bare feet to head downstairs to the kitchen.

She moved at a snail's pace about the kitchen until she had fixed and enjoyed a full cup of strong coffee, extra sweet with lots of cream. Her twins liked to tease that she liked a splash of coffee in her cup of milk.

Zaria leaned back against the counter, her eyes shifting to the round table in the center of the breakfast nook. She felt a little melancholy as she was filled with memories of her girls when they were just eight years old, with their heads buried in their books as they did their homework at that table every day after school. Now they were finishing up their sophomore year at Denmark Tech with their own apartment down the block from the campus.

She wished they could have come home, with her having a rare weekend off from work, but her girls were deep into studying for their finals. So, Zaria was alone in the big house. All weekend.

She bit her bottom lip and furrowed her brow.

Her house was clean. There were no chores to be done. No big meals to be cooked. No yard to be raked or tended.

So many things about Zaria's life had changed. Many, many things.

Many things *had* to change.

"Thank God," she muttered, quickly fixing herself another cup of coffee before she made her way back upstairs to her bedroom.

Her cell phone was vibrating like a sex toy, and she nearly tripped over a three-inch-heeled bootie lying on the floor, having to steady her cup to keep from spilling her coffee as she rushed across the room to grab the phone. "Hello," she said breathlessly.

"Ummm . . . Zaria?"

She smiled as she set her coffee cup on the nightstand. "Nigel." She sighed in pleasure, thinking of the tall and slender West Indian she met a few months ago at a Caribbean festival in Charleston. The College of Charleston grad student was handsome and smart and funny . . . and just shy of twenty-five.

He laughed. "I thought I dialed the wrong number," he said.

At the thought of spending the rest of her long weekend alone around her house, Zaria was glad for a little friendly diversion. "No, you got me."

"You're not busy?" he asked, surprised.

"Nope." She stood up and sucked in her stomach, turning her head to eye her side profile in the mirror.

"Must be my lucky day."

Zaria walked over to her closet. "Or mine," she said.

Beep.

"Then let's spend the day together," he offered.

Zaria reached for an oversized straw hat, plopping it onto her head. "A nice day at the beach sounds like a plan," she suggested, knowing her wish was his command.

It always was.

Beep.

Zaria frowned at the steady beep signaling another call coming in.

"When and where should I pick you up?" he asked.

She looked at her phone. It was her supervisor from the restaurant bar where she worked. "Hold on one sec," she said, putting Nigel on hold as she answered the other line.

"Zaria, I hate to do this. I know this is your weekend off—"

"You need me to work," she said, cutting to the chase and skipping the BS.

"We need you in an hour."

She shook her head as she took the hat off her head and set it back on the shelf . . . along with her plans for a fun day with a sexy young man willing to please.

Chapter 2

Kaleb Strong leaned his broad and muscular back against the porch railing and pretended to look off into the distance at the vast lands of the Strong Ranch. Having spent all of his childhood and a good part of his adult years on the ranch, he knew it like the back of his hand—every bit of the hundreds of acres. But he preferred to look out at the barn and paddocks and beyond to pretend like he didn't feel like a fifth wheel.

His mom had cooked a big meal in honor of his dad's birthday. They had enjoyed their feast of barbecued ribs, collard greens and rice, and macaroni and cheese. Now they lounged on his parents' sizable front porch, enjoying the mild heat of late spring—his eldest brother, Kade, and his wife, Garcelle; his brother Kahron and his wife, Bianca; and his brother Kaeden and his fiancée, Jade. All were sitting beside their loves in that comfortable and easy way of people who adored each other. Even his parents, Lisha and

Kael, were sitting side by side in their oversized black rockers like two peas in a pod.

And that left him sitting alone and looking like Only the Lonely.

Their baby sister, Kaitlyn, was away for the week on a cruise to Brazil with her friends and wasn't there to break up the feeling of a huge group date. Even his niece, Kadina, and his nephews, KJ and Karlos, were all napping inside the house and unable to serve as buffers to the love fest surrounding him.

All of his brothers had found the loves of their lives. They were clearly on the path to that long-lasting relationship that their parents had. Even Kaeden.

Kaleb looked back over his broad shoulder at his brother, who was warily eyeing a bee flying about the porch. Kaeden was allergic to any and everything outdoors. He was the only one in the family who didn't work on a ranch. Instead he was a successful accountant who handled all of the paperwork for their various ranches, plus he did the accounting for many businesses and corporations in the surrounding areas.

And unlike his brothers, Kaeden had never shown that cocky bravado when it came to women. Between Kahron, Kade, and himself, they had enjoyed their share of beautiful women, but Kaeden had always been reserved and cautious around women. At times even clumsy.

Kaleb shifted his deep-set eyes over to his brother's fiancée, Jade. She was the epitome of a beautiful woman. All curves and prettiness and sex appeal. The temptation of her honey had made him one of the many men of Holtsville buzzing around her skirts. While she swatted him away along with the rest, Jade had handed over the entire pot to his brother.

And she was completely in love with Kaeden.

Smiling, he shook his head as he looked away from them. There was a time when he would have given his right hand to spend a hot night in the woods with Jade, but those feelings vanished the moment she made her choice. Now, one year later, he looked at her with the same fondness as Garcelle and Bianca—and wished to have a woman just like them in his own life.

The quantity of women was not his problem—he was more of a connoisseur of fine females than any of his brothers. His mother always admonished him the hardest for being a playboy—or man-whore as she liked to say. Kaleb's problem was the quality of women who filled his mental black book—or rather the quality of his relationships with them. He should start trying dinner and a movie rather than staying in the bedroom and using a six-pack of Magnums. Or at least have the dinner and a movie *first.*

The sudden wail of the baby from the monitor caused everyone to jump in surprise.

Garcelle rose from her spot next to Kade on the top step of the porch. "Our *bebé* is awake from his nap," she said, her Spanish accent prominent.

"*Bebé*? Karlos just turned one a few months ago and he's almost as big as KJ," Kahron joked, the laughter in his eyes hidden behind his shades.

Everyone on the porch laughed, including

Kade and Garcelle before she excused herself to walk into the house.

"Kade was big and sturdy like that too," Kael said, flipping the pages of the *Press and Standard* newspaper. "He looked like a six-month-old when he was born."

Lisha nodded and comically winced as she rocked in her chair. "Thank the heavens the rest of my children got smaller and not bigger," she said, looking over at Kade's six-foot-nine frame and winking at him.

Kael snorted in derision. "Thank the heavens everything snapped back into place."

"Oh, man, come on, Daddy, man," Kaleb moaned, frowning deeply as everyone else on the porch groaned.

He lowered the newspaper with an innocent expression on his square and handsome face. "What?"

Lisha just chuckled softly as she reached over to lightly pat and squeeze his upper thigh. They exchanged a long look.

It was a look he had seen them share many times over the years. Kaleb wanted to feel everything that was layered in that look: the love, the desire, the trust, and the commitment. He had been raised in a home filled with loving parents. How could he help but want the same for himself?

Kade's teenaged daughter, Kadina, stepped out onto the porch, holding a fidgety Karlos in her arms. Garcelle held the screen door open as little KJ, Bianca and Kahron's toddler, stepped down onto the porch.

Kaleb instantly felt his heart surge at the sight

of his niece and nephews. He couldn't help but wonder if any of the three would inherit the Strong trait of their hair prematurely turning gray. Even his sister had a thick streak of silver in the front of her hair that she dyed jet black.

"Bring me Bam-Bam," Kaleb requested, using his nickname for the baby, his strong and muscled arms already lifting as KJ waddled his three-year-old body to his mother, Bianca.

"Gladly," Kadina said wryly, her sleek ponytail swinging in the air as she whirled to walk her little brother over to him. "He is *so* heavy that it's not even funny."

"He's going to be big and strong like his uncle Kaleb," he said, taking the smiling baby to stand up on his thigh as he bounced him on his knee. "Ain't that right, man."

Karlos cooed and giggled, releasing a small spit bubble that popped and lightly wet his cheeks. He could already see the Strong features in his nephew's face. He knew the rounded cheeks would become lean with high cheekbones and his jaw would square, just like all the other Strong men. *Will my son look like him?* Kaleb wondered.

His eyes narrowed as he shifted his gaze back out to the vast acres of the farm. He was a grown-ass man ready for some grown-man changes . . . *with* the right woman.

Kaleb focused his deep-set eyes on his nephew as small and pudgy hands began to pat against his cheeks.

"You look real good with a baby, Kaleb."

He looked up to find Jade, Garcelle, Bianca,

and his mom standing in a semicircle around him. Kaleb leaned back a bit from them.

"Uh-oh," one of the men said from behind the curtain the women's bodies made.

Kaleb's brows furrowed as he locked eyes with each one.

"You know my friend Lizbeth would be perfect for you," Bianca said with a wink that twinkled brighter than the diamond hoop earrings dangling from her ears.

"Or," Garcelle added as she motioned with her finger and eyed the other women, "Amanda from my pediatrician's office is a-*doh*-rable."

Jade frowned and shook her head. "No, no, no. I know her and the Amanda at work is totally different from the Amanda after hours. DRAMA."

"Scratch her, then," Lisha said emphatically.

Bianca shifted KJ up higher on her hip. "What about Yolanda, the new choir director at church—"

"Okay, ladies," Kaleb said, rising to his feet and handing the baby to Garcelle. "Thank you for your concern, but I'm straight. Trust me. I don't need help with my love life—"

"Maybe not your sex life but you need some help with your love life," Garcelle drawled.

"Sex and love are two different things, son," Lisha said, reaching out to pat the side of his strong face. "One involves the heart and the other involves your—"

Kaleb pretended to gag. "Okay, I'm not discussing sex with my moms," he said, easing between Bianca and Jade to free himself. His brothers and father all cast amused glances at him, and Kaleb glared at them as if they were buzzards circling his dying body.

They all chuckled.

Their mother was infamous for pinning one or all of them down with questions, commentary, and opinions. Now that she had backup from her sons' wives and fiancée, she was *really* unstoppable.

Brrrrnnnggg.

Kaleb grabbed his cell phone from the clip on his belt, more than glad for the diversion. "Yeah," he said, turning his broad back on his entire family.

"Where you at?"

Kaleb frowned at the male voice, pulling the phone away from his ear to look at the number on the caller ID. He didn't recognize it. "Who is this?"

"Orion. I'm on my brother's phone."

He nodded in clarity. "Oh. Whassup?"

"Yo, my little brother done messed up and got engaged and I'm taking him out tonight. You down?"

Kaleb immediately had a vision of red lights, bare breasts, gyrating hips, and dollar bills. He began to shake his head before the words even left his lips. "Nah, man. I have some work to do on my farm early in the morning. No T and A for me tonight."

"T and A?" someone muttered, before all of the women behind him either hummed in disapproval or sucked air between their teeth. Again the men chuckled.

"It's a bunch of us headed right to a sports bar

in Charleston to grab a few drinks and something to eat. Nothing major."

"I can call Suzi over right now. Poor thing is always sitting at home alone. I'm sure they'll hit it off."

Kaleb stiffened and his mouth froze as the whisper from behind his back reached his ear. "Actually, I just need to go home and change," he said, immediately deciding that of his options of a lonely night at home mulling over just how lonely his home was, staying at his parents' for a matchmaking session that smelled like it could go horribly wrong in an instant, or heading out to a sports bar, he was choosing the latter.

"We'll pick you up at your place on the way to Charleston . . . in an hour."

"A'ight." Kaleb closed his phone and slid it back into its clip before adjusting his shoulders and expanding his broad chest in the charcoal gray Dickies uniform shirt he wore.

"You going, Kaleb?" Lisha asked, with a lengthy sidelong glance as KJ came up to stand before her with a smile.

Kaleb scratched at his chin, feeling the bristly beginnings of a shadow. He had to shave daily to keep away his shadow and could have grown a full beard in less than a week. His brothers used to tease him as a teenager that he was a werewolf. "In a little bit," he finally said.

"Got plans?" she asked, not at all good at being subtle.

He chuckled before turning to lean against the railing and look over at her. "Orion's little brother just got engaged, and a bunch of the fellas are going to a sports bar to have a few drinks and celebrate with him."

"Tevon?" Kaeden asked. "He's marrying . . . *Melissa*?"

The men all exchanged long looks and Kaleb just shrugged. He knew exactly what they were thinking. To most men, there were two types of women: the kind you bed and the kind you wed. With her history and fondness for men, Melissa was far from the latter, but to each his own. *Maybe* Tevon knew something they didn't. Maybe not. Kaleb wasn't about to judge.

"Don't worry, Uncle Kaleb. I understand," Kadina said, nearly as tall as his shoulder. "You can't look for love. You have to wait for it to find you."

"Really?" he asked, looking down as she wrapped her slender arm around his waist. He was ever and always amazed that she was sprouting up so fast. *What happened to the cute, pudgy kid with those fuzzy ponytails?* "Just as long as love isn't looking for you, kid."

Kadina playfully rolled her eyes heavenward. "Oh, Uncle Kaleb, you sound like Daddy . . . and Uncle Kahron . . . and Uncle Kaeden . . . and Grandpa."

Kaleb nodded like there wasn't anything wrong with that. "We're men. We know what little boys are thinking . . . and wanting . . . and plotting," he warned her, reaching up to pull her ponytail.

"I know, I know."

With one quick kiss to her forehead, Kaleb raised his hand to the rest of his family on the porch. "Gotta go. See y'all tomorrow," he said over his broad shoulder, already jogging down the stairs in his well-worn Timberlands. The Strong men were ranchers, but it was all about Dickies uniforms and Timberland boots instead of Wrangler jeans, spurs, and Stetsons. A new breed of cowboy for sure.

"You don't want to take a plate?" his mother called out as he climbed into his rusted red work truck.

"No, ma'am," he called back in his deep voice before turning the key that he'd left in the ignition.

With one blast of the horn, Kaleb headed down the long road that would take him home to prepare for a rare night out with the fellas. But the closer he got to home and the more he thought about how early he had to rise in the morning to work his farm, Kaleb followed his gut and called Orion to cancel his plans.

A night home alone was no biggie.

CHAPTER 3

Two weeks later

Kaleb inhaled deeply of the steam swirling around his nude form as he leaned forward against the tiled shower wall and let the spray beat down against his back. The streams flowed across his hard, square buttocks and farther down to the backs of his muscled legs. He rested his head against the forearm he pressed to the slick, wet wall. He had already washed off every bit of the sweat and grime from a hard day's work, helping his farmhands herd his seventy head of cattle to graze in one of the ten paddocks on the thirty acres of his land he'd sectioned off just for grazing.

But Kaleb remained in the shower, knowing that he was stalling.

The night of his father's birthday dinner, he'd gone home and slumped down in his favorite recliner in front of the television. And he flipped through the channels. And flipped some more.

Eventually the sight of a pretty, dark-skinned beauty had caught his attention and he paused to watch the movement of her full lips as she spoke. Eventually her words began to filter through his fascination with her look. She was a relationship "expert" giving out advice on finding the love of your life.

If you can admit that a lot of your relationships ended because of your own inability to be one hundred percent present in your relationship, consider that you may have had a relationship that could have been successful if your goals and motivations were different.

Her words came back to him as he finally turned off the shower, pushed aside the ebony shower curtain, and stepped out. He barely covered his damp nakedness with a towel as he crossed the spacious tiled bathroom into his unkempt bedroom. His clothes were already laid out across his unmade bed. His hair was freshly cut. His beard eradicated. His hygiene was on point.

Date time?

"I'd rather milk all my cows by hand by my damn self," Kaleb muttered as he used the towel to blot the last of the beads of water from his deep bronzed skin. Fine thick hairs covered his chest and feathered down to narrow between the hard groove of his six-pack before spreading out to surround his now limp but heavy dick swinging across the top of his thighs as he moved.

Kaleb grabbed a pair of clean boxers from the basket of clothes he still needed to fold—or at least shove into the drawers of his dresser. He was just grateful he'd remembered to toss a load of clothes into the wash last night. He was a bachelor living alone in a three-bedroom home and putting most of the hours of his workdays into keeping his farm successful. Kahron swore that Kaleb needed to follow his lead and hire a maid, but Kaleb caught enough hell keeping his mother from showing up with her cleaning supplies. No maids.

Keeping an eye on the time displayed on his digital cable box, he hurried into his clothes, which were freshly dry-cleaned. With a quick double spritz of cologne on his neck, Kaleb grabbed his wallet and keys from atop the loose change scattered on his dresser.

Moving quickly, because he hated to be late, Kaleb strode out of the room and across the long, narrow hall into the open, spacious area housing the living room, den, dining room, and kitchen. His footsteps echoed across the tiled floor as he reached the oversized front door. Once in his car and headed up the highway, he thought twice about even going through with the date.

If you can admit that a lot of your relationships ended because of your own inability to be one hundred percent present in your relationship, consider that you may have had a relationship that could have been successful if your goals and motivations were different.

For the last two weeks, he had gone through his extensive list of exes and tried to consider which could have been the love of his life. He could admit that a long-term relationship hadn't been any part of the equation for him.

Had he overlooked Mrs. Right because his high sex drive had him keeping his eye on—and his dick in—Mrs. Right for My Bed?

One date a night on top of the rigorous work on his dairy farm and he was mentally worn out and physically feeling the effects of heavy meals and lack of sleep—and lack of evidence that he had overlooked the woman he was meant to spend the rest of his life with.

Tonight?

As he pulled into the front yard, Kaleb fixed his ebony eyes on the door of the single-wide trailer with pink shutters. His ex, Yvette. He released a heavy breath as her front door opened and she stepped out onto the top of the small stoop with a soft smile.

Could the soft-spoken kindergarten teacher he'd dated a few times a few years ago be the one?

Two hours later, Kaleb pressed his elbows against the table as he fought like hell to keep his eyes open. Some of his fatigue was the full day they'd spent moving the fences around the paddocks they were ready to graze for the next month, but the majority was because he had zoned out on the date fifteen minutes in. Yvette was bossy and demanding, as if he were one of her kindergarteners.

"Kaleb, it really is not good manners to place your elbows on the table," she said, and then gave him that soft smile that irked the hell out of his nerves.

His eyes squinted as he continued to watch her while she pierced his naughty elbows with her eyes.

Kaleb was beginning to wonder what the qualifications were of the sexy expert from the television besides looking yummy enough to attract any man her heart desired.

While Yvette explained proper etiquette to him, no words from her mouth reached his ears. He was pretty good at tuning people out—something that used to frustrate his parents when he was a child and wanting to annoy them.

As he replayed in his mind the string of dates he'd had over the last two weeks, he visualized the face of every woman as if their head were morphing like those in that Michael Jackson "Black or White" video.

Veronica, the pretty real estate agent with the naturally curly long lashes: "Kaleb, I need a man to focus his all on me. It's 2011 and I'm not taking any shorts. It's all or nothing, baby." *Nothing. Next!*

Malika, the sassy Walmart cashier with long nails and even longer braids. "Don't you think you should dye your hair?" she had asked, twirling one of her talons in the direction of his head. *Whoa. Next!*

Jhavon, the full-figured widow who was a whiz at tongue tricks. "Listen, there's no need to lie. Me and my kids missed you, Kaleb," she said, rubbing circles on the palm of his hand. *And that was five kids. How could he forget them? ALL FIVE of them? Next!*

Anna, the nurse with soft eyes and an even softer touch. "So the therapist said I was finally over my ex and am ready to move on to a new relationship. And then you called. It's fate. I think we were really meant to be together forever. Right?" *Wrong. Next!*

And Francine, the agile attorney with a round face and large features that were usually angelic. "So you think every woman falls for the sexy-farmer thing and just lets you hit and split, huh?" she had asked sharply. "And you ask me out to dinner two years later, and I should be happy to be graced with your presence, huh?" *Uh-oh! Next!*

And a few more disasters he refused to dwell on.

The point was, none of them were his idea of the one.

"Kaleb! Your elbows. My goodness," Yvette said through clenched teeth, glancing around at the other diners as if they, too, were looking at his elbows on the table in reproach.

"Yes, they are *my* elbows," he stressed. "My almost-thirty-year-old elbows to go along with my almost-thirty-year-old behind that doesn't need to be treated like a preschooler."

She dramatically inhaled a deep breath as she leaned back and looked at him with her mouth open in what could only be indignation.

Kaleb raised his hand. "Teacher, may I get a hall pass to go to the bathroom?" he said, his deep tones tinged with sarcasm.

Her bottom lip dropped another inch.

Kaleb stood and made his way across the crowded seafood restaurant to the restroom, needing a moment away from her more than anything. He actually felt bad about being rude, but her "do this, don't do that" manner really grated on his patience. Still, he knew she deserved an apology and a better attitude from him. Those things she would most definitely receive. Another call from him? That was a negative.

"Excuse me."

Kaleb turned his head and looked down at the sound of a woman's voice behind him. His eyes landed directly on a full bosom in a crisp white dress shirt with an opening that exposed creamy brown flesh and a diamond-encrusted heart pendant snuggled in cleavage.

He jerked his eyes up . . . and met a pair of twinkling and amused eyes that were filled with laughter. An energy radiated between them and made him feel light-headed in just an instant.

"Enjoy the view?" she asked with a slight arch of her brow, before she continued past him into the crowded lobby.

His mouth fell open a bit as he watched the way she moved with confidence, her sequin heels peeking out beneath the wide-legged black slacks she wore. She was tall. Very tall. And curvaceous. Everything about her was soft—but not sloppy. Firm and curvy.

She looked back over her shoulder and their eyes met.

Kaleb felt like a strong hand punched him in the gut and then squeezed his heart in a fist as his eyes took her in. She was really pretty with high cheekbones and full lips. Her eyes were filled with fun and laughter. She smiled at him, and her face went from pretty to radiant.

The crowd shifted and she was gone from his sight.

Kaleb felt disappointed that the moment had passed.

"Kaleb."

He turned in surprise to find Yvette standing behind him with her pocketbook swinging on her thin shoulder. "Obviously this little reunion isn't working, and there's no need for us to have an uncomfortable forty-five-minute ride back to Holtsville, so my father is here to pick me up." She nodded toward the door.

"That was fast," he said, looking back down at her.

"My parents live in the apartment complex around the corner," she said before moving past him.

"Listen, Yvette, I'm sorry about snapping at you at the table—"

"I accept your apology," she said stiffly over her shoulder, steadily walking toward the door. "Good-bye, Kaleb."

Thinking it sounded more like *good riddance* than *good-bye,* Kaleb walked back to the table to pay the bill and tip their waiter before he turned and *finally* made his way to the restroom to relieve himself.

Zaria smiled at the elderly couple as they rose from their bar stools to go and claim their table in the restaurant. She picked up their half-empty glasses, emptying the contents in the sink before placing the glasses in the tray for the busboy to retrieve.

The restaurant was packed, and a lot of the

overflow was spilling into the bar. She had barely wiped down the wood in front of the vacated spots before another couple occupied the bar stools.

"Good evening. What can I get for you?" Zaria asked, setting small square napkins in front of each of them.

"I'll have Absolut straight on the rocks," the man said.

The woman leaned against her man's arm possessively. "A glass of Moscato."

"Coming right up," Zaria said, fighting the urge to tell the woman, "Baby, I do NOT want your man."

It was clear the woman took one look at Zaria and assumed (1) she wanted him and (2) she had what it took to get him.

Zaria could only shake her head as she poured their drinks. The last thing she would ever want to do is share a man. The pickings were not that slim, and her values were not invisible. Discovering there was another person in your relationship had a way of making the idea of being a side chick distasteful.

She wasn't going to do unto others what was done to her. No haps.

Zaria made sure to keep a polite but distant smile on her face as she set their drinks and their bill before them. He paid and tipped her well.

"Thank you," she said warmly, then moved away from him and his scowling woman.

Zaria motioned to the restaurant owner that she needed a bathroom break. He finished what he was doing and came over to relieve her. As she made her way around the bar, a glint of silver hair caught her eye. She assumed the broad shoulders belonged to a fit elderly man until she eased through the people in the crowded lobby and lightly touched his back as she tried to pass him. "Excuse me," she said, feeling the definition of his muscles beneath the navy and white checkered shirt he wore. *Do Grandpa!*

She looked up as he looked down over his broad shoulder. His eyes fell directly to her cleavage. She studied his features, more than intrigued at the sight of his youthful, handsome, and sculptured face framed by a low-cut fade of his silver-flecked hair. He could be no more than thirty—if that. He was prematurely gray and it worked for him.

As did the deep-set ebony eyes above high, warriorlike cheekbones and a square chin with a strong nose straight from the motherland. The hardness of his beauty was softened only by the feminine length and curl of his lashes. A small and jagged scar on his cheek did nothing to deter from his looks.

The warmth of his muscular frame seemed to radiate through her hand and then course over her body until she tingled in awareness. Her pulse. Her nipples. The now-throbbing bud snuggled deeply within her thick lips below.

He looked up at her face and their eyes met.

Something unspoken and palpable happened between them. Something fierce and quickly moving. Something unlike anything she had ever felt before.

Not even with her husband.

"Enjoy the view?" she asked him, reaching for

frivolity to break the moment, slightly arching her brow.

Breaking the stare and quickly removing her hand, she continued past him and through the crowd to the hall leading to the restrooms. She was still a bit flustered by her instant reaction to the man, feeling nervous and anxious. Just before she entered the lavatory, she looked back for him. He was gone.

His image was clearly embedded in her memory. The feel of his body under her hand. The subtle but sexy scent of his cologne and natural scent blending in the air around him. He was sexy and silver. Interesting. Damn interesting.

"Mmm, mmm, mmm." Zaria fanned herself as she entered one of the many stalls.

Minutes later, she left the stall and washed her hands thoroughly at one of the bowl sinks. She dried them with hand towels before she readjusted her clothing in the mirror.

Her uniform of white shirt and black slacks left a lot to be desired. If it wasn't a requirement for her position as a bartender, she would burn the pants and wear only the shirt, open with a white tank underneath. But c'est la vie.

She did what she had to do to make a living. And she had to work.

Her ex-husband, Ned, wasn't a wealthy man who could afford enough alimony for her to continue being a stay-at-home mother—especially when their children were over eighteen and in college. She was awarded some alimony and the house—with the remaining mortgage payment to go along with it. It was either that or she moved out and accepted a buyout offer from Ned, or she sold the house and split the profits—if any. She chose to keep it and fight like hell to pay for it.

Besides, after a quarter of a lifetime being a stay-at-home wife and mother who got blindsided by love and life, she wanted to be out of the house working and living the life she had put on hold.

She was just over forty, and entering college left no time to work to pay bills.

She barely knew how to open the e-mails her girls insisted on sending her, and she didn't want to be inside an office all day.

She didn't want to learn how to run a register, or wait tables, or clean hospitals, or anything else for that matter.

Zaria wanted to do something she liked doing and knew she would have fun doing it. She loved clubbing, looking sexy, and after a night of harmless flirting with a sexy bartender, she decided *that's* what she wanted to do!

Thankfully she had a lot of fun learning to mix drinks during the two-week course, and "studying" with sexy Halil. Every time she crushed ice, she had to make herself not think of the tricks he could do with an ice cube. He and that ice trick had been her eye-opener to the wonderful world of younger men.

Taking a deep breath, Zaria smoothed her hair behind her ears, her oversized crystal inside-out hoops flashing in the lights above. "Just one more hour," she told her reflection, then left the restroom.

She made her way back to the bar, reclaiming her spot from the owner, who look relieved. She smiled at all her patrons as she checked to make sure everyone had a drink before them.

Zaria had just slid a Mojito in front of a suit-clad middle-aged man when a flash of silver showed in her peripheral vision. She turned. Sure enough, it was Sexy Silver walking from the restrooms toward the front doors of the restaurant. Her eyes dipped to take in his bowlegged walk.

He looked up suddenly and directly at her, his steps becoming hesitant before he nodded briefly and continued out the door alone.

Zaria could easily see him being one of her Hot Boyz—her nickname for the younger men in her life who were sexy as all get-out and just as eager to keep a smile on her face. *They aim to please,* she thought saucily with a little mischief filling her eyes.

"Zaria, I'm out, girl."

She looked over her shoulder at Pat, one of the waitresses, standing at the end of the bar. "Lucky you," she said, eyeing the measure of triple sec she poured into the heavy-duty blender.

"I'm going home to change and then head to Club Energy," she said, leaning her elbows on the bar as she played with her micro braids. "You know Trey Songz is performing, girl."

Zaria visualized the sexy young'un with the sultry voice. "Mr. Invented Sex, huh?" she asked.

Pat nodded. "If one drop of sweat falls off his body, I will be front and center to catch it in my mouth."

Zaria frowned playfully. "That serious, huh?"

"Most def."

Zaria laughed. "Club Energy, huh? I might

come," she said, focusing on pouring tequila into the blender.

Suddenly the soft baby hairs on her nape tingled as if lightly touched. Her intuition told her that someone was behind her, watching her, causing a slight shift in the energy around her body. And she knew. She knew before she even lifted her eyes to the mirror that *he* would be in the reflection.

Her heart swelled as her pulse shifted into overdrive.

There he stood at the bar. The reflection of his body was right over her shoulder as if he stood directly behind her. She couldn't lie. They looked good together. Damn good.

Their eyes locked and that vibe was there. It was hard to ignore, and again it was a surprise to her mind and body. A surprise . . . but not a disturbance. Nothing negative or wrong or foreign. Not at all.

"Zaria, my drinks ready?" one of the waitresses asked.

Unfortunately, she jumped in surprise and accidentally punched the button to start the blender without putting the cover on. The liquid contents sprayed up into her face. She let loose a high-pitched squeal, turned off the blender, and jumped back all at once. "Dammit," she swore under her breath, using a napkin to wipe the errant liquid from her face, careful not to wipe off or smudge her makeup.

"I'll make you a fresh drink," Zaria told the waitress.

As she dumped the contents of the pitcher

and started over, she was aware of Sexy Silver now sitting at the bar watching her every move. He was controlling their interaction, and that was a no-no for her. She was used to younger men being discombobulated by her.

She was nervous. Anxious. Aware of him.

"I'll be right with you," she said, noticing how his massive biceps strained against the short sleeve of his shirt.

"No problem," he answered with a nod.

It seemed like an eternity before she finally pushed the two frozen margaritas toward the waitress. "Sorry about that," she said with a soft smile.

Sexy Silver's eyes were resting on her, and she knew—just as sure as she knew her mama's name—that he had doubled back for her and not for a drink. That flustered her even more, and she felt as if she were walking the edge of a cliff with clown shoes on.

"And what can I get for you?" she asked him as she walked up to stand before him.

"Your name and number so that I can call you," he said with confidence, tapping his fingertips against the top of the bar.

Zaria fought the urge to lean against the bar to be closer to him. The restaurant owner had a zero-tolerance policy against fraternizing with the patrons. "Just like that, huh?" she asked, fighting the urge to rub her hand atop his to stop the incessant drumming . . . and to touch him. Feel him. Experience him.

Mmm, mmm, mmm.

"Hell, I want that too," one of the men at the end of the bar said loudly.

Zaria saw Kaleb look down at him.

Uh-oh. "Well, gentlemen," she said, addressing both, "the owner—my boss—doesn't allow any of the workers to fraternize with guests, so that's a polite no to both of you," she said, gently using the rule that usually irritated the hell out of her.

Kaleb nodded in understanding as he rose to his feet. "Too bad," he said, reaching out briefly to touch her hand. "I don't want you to get in trouble."

Zaria thought about never seeing him again. It didn't sit right with her. But she didn't want to cause a brawl, and the other man was looking on intently. "Thank you," she said.

"I gotta go see my cousin Trey anyway," he said before turning and walking out of the bar and out of her life.

Kaleb jumped to his feet as soon as she walked past security and into the dimly lit interior of Club Energy. After almost an hour and a half and two beers and six glasses of ice water, there she was. His eyes skimmed her body in her white shirt and black pants. Nothing could take away from appeal. The ample curve of her bosom. The long length of her legs. The wide breadth of her hips. Hips manufactured just for a man's grasp to pull her lower body closer . . . and closer . . .

The music in the club was almost deafening as Zaria entered the double-level hot spot. She paused, looking through those dancing, those holding up the wall, and those just lounging with drinks at their tables watching the action.

Security let her know she had already missed Trey Songz' performance, but that was fine because she was looking for another young and fine man with a body built to please.

There was sudden movement by the bar and she turned that way. *I found him,* she thought, her face lighting with a smile as she notched her head higher and made her way toward him.

They met somewhere in the middle of the distance between them. They both smiled at each other as the colored lights reflected on and off their faces, breaking up the darkness around them.

"I didn't think you got my hidden message about coming here," he said, following pure instinct and want by pressing his large and strong hands on her hips to pull her closer.

She shivered from his touch, bringing her hand up to grip his strong biceps through his shirt. "I almost didn't," she admitted.

"I'm Kaleb Strong, by the way."

"Zaria. Zaria Ali."

"Nice to meet you."

"Same here."

Four hours later, Kaleb lifted Zaria's body up against his, before turning to press her back against the front door of her home. As he brought his hands down to cup her full buttocks, he brought his face in close to hers.

Zaria tightened her hold around his neck, feeling secure in his embrace as her eyes flitted over his face as if memorizing every detail. She tilted her chin up to trace the full outline of his mouth with the tip of her tongue, enjoying the way her body trembled. She laughed huskily as he pressed his mouth to the corner of hers. "Things are going so fast," she whispered against his lips.

Kaleb leaned back to look down at her, liking how the porch light reflected like twinkling stars in her eyes. "We don't have to do this," he told her. Still he wanted her to *want* this moment.

He eased his hands up under her shirt to press against the warm skin of her waist and stepped back to let her down onto her feet.

She shook her head. "It feels like we have to," she admitted, speaking her feelings. Her body felt alive and vibrant. His touch was like pure energy. His body like the most solid of foundations.

She kissed him again, deepening their connection as she pressed her tongue into his mouth to lightly stroke his own.

He moaned in regret when she turned in his embrace, pressing her head to the door as his hands came up to massage her aching nipples beneath her shirt. His hardness ached from wanting her as he fought the urge to press the length of it against her buttocks. Instead he shifted her hair and placed a hot kiss on her neck. "I want you," he moaned against her ear.

Zaria felt completely light-headed and hot and

flustered as she took her key from her pocket and unlocked the front door. Stepping away from him, she went inside the house and began to unbutton her shirt. "Come and get me," she said.

Kaleb's gut clenched as he stepped inside with his dick leading the way back to her. He used his foot to soundly close the door behind him.

CHAPTER 4

Zaria let her shirt fall to the floor in a puddle as Kaleb came forward and began to unbutton his shirt. He pulled it and his white tee over his head. She watched him closely as she hit the switch to bask the foyer with some soft light from above. She loved the smooth, flat hair covering his well-defined chest, the narrowing of his waist, and the hardness of his abdomen. The muscles of his arms flexed as he removed his pants and boxers.

"What exactly do you do to get a body like that?" Zaria asked as she stepped out of her pants and stood before him in a matching bra and panty set that was pure black lace and barely there.

Kaleb paused. His eyes locked on her. "Huh?"

Zaria laughed and eased her thumbs into the rim of her low-slung bikinis to pull them farther down on her hips until the top of her plump and bald mound was exposed.

Kaleb's hooded eyes dropped to take in the move, to enjoy the tempting sight. "Shit," he swore.

Zaria laughed low in her throat. "Focus, sugar,"

she said teasingly as his dick lengthened away from his body.

Kaleb wrapped one strong hand around the thick base of his dick and cut his eyes up to her as he stroked it. "You focus, darling," he countered with a wicked smile.

Zaria removed her thumbs, causing the bands of the bikini to lightly snap against her body. She tilted her head to the side as she unhooked her bra and removed it, slowly letting it dangle from her finger. She felt her dark nipples harden in the cool air-conditioned room as she moved her shoulders back and forth to make the plump mounds jiggle a bit. The look on her face said *touché.*

"I'm all out of clothes, so you win," he said, taking long strides and strokes to reach her.

Zaria worked her bikinis over her hips and then down her legs, kicking them away and standing before him naked. "I'm all out of clothes, so now *you* win."

"Wow," Kaleb said, drawing it out as his eyes took in the small star tattoo just above her plump and shaven V-shaped mound. Her body was amazing. Soft and curvy. Her breasts were full and heavy, not the Barbie-like stiff cones that defied gravity and reality. Her waist dipped in to help create the hourglass shape, but she lacked flat or six-packed abs that resembled his. Her legs were shapely and well toned but womanly.

Not the athletic build of a woman tied to her gym membership.

His dick hardened even more in his grasp.

Zaria turned and walked to the doorway of her bedroom. She looked over her shoulder at him.

"I need to take a shower. Coming?" she asked, continuing into her bedroom, already knowing he was right behind her.

Still, the sudden smack on her ass surprised her.

The steam swirled around the shower stall as Kaleb enjoyed the feel of the hot water streaming against his back as he held Zaria's face.

She smiled against his lips. "Do I look like Aunt Jemima with this scarf on?"

Kaleb lowered his forehead to hers with a chuckle. "No, but I wondered what the purpose was," he admitted. "I would love to stand under the water with you and kiss you—"

Zaria looked alarmed. "I'm not getting my hair wet!"

Kaleb shook his head, smiling down at her and thinking she looked really pretty. "Don't you have a hair dryer?"

"I wear weave—I don't do them," she said softly, her eyes twinkling as they continued to look at each other.

"That's not your real hair?" Kaleb asked in disbelief.

Zaria laughed softly and shook her head. She reached up to stroke one of his hands before turning her face to kiss the center of his palm, then guiding it down her body to press against her breast. She shivered at the feel of his hands—the kind of rough hands of a man who worked hard for his money—against her flesh. "This is real," she whispered as the steam rose between them.

Zaria guided his hand down her back to press

against her fleshy backside. "And that's real," she moaned, lifting her head to expose her neck to his warm kisses.

Kaleb bent his fingers to tighten the grip, almost possessively. He moaned before he licked a trail from her chin to her collarbone.

Zaria felt weak. She shivered. "And this? This is very real," she whispered into the steam as she eased his hand between her thighs to press against her moist lips. Her clit ached and she felt the wetness of her core as it pulsated thickly.

Kaleb massaged her swollen clit in a smooth circle before easing his index finger up inside her.

"Ah," Zaria cried out sharply, arching her back and bringing both hands up to clutch blindly at his broad shoulders.

Kaleb brought his arm around her waist to hold her damp and trembling body securely as he stroked his fingers inside her moist, hot, and rigid walls.

Quickly—too quickly—Zaria felt that anxious shimmy through her body that alerted her she was about to climax. "No, don't make me come," she begged against his wet neck. "Not yet."

Kaleb had to fight like hell to stop stroking her. He wanted her to come. He wanted to feel her release, see the rapture on her face and hear it in her cries. In that moment, he wanted that more than anything else in the world. Anything.

"Damn, we shoulda brought condoms in here," he told her, lifting his head to look at her.

"Then let's get to the condom," Zaria said.

Finally, and with much reluctance, he freed his finger and used his now-free hand to open the glass shower door. He scooped her up into his arms and stepped out of the stall, surrounded by steam.

Zaria wrapped her arms around his neck as she pressed kisses to his strong neck, enjoying the scent of soap clinging to his skin as closely as she clung to him. He laid her down in the middle of her bed, looking down at her body as if he wished he could remember that moment forever and making her feel the same.

"I'll be right back," Kaleb said, turning to stride out of the room as if he wasn't as naked as the day he was born, with his manhood pointing away from his body like a fifth appendage. A very large appendage.

Zaria stretched out in the middle of the bed, lifting her arms high above her head to untie the scarf and fling it over the bed to float to the floor. She fought the urge to rush back to the dressing table in her bathroom to slap on some lip gloss and a coat of mascara. And good thing because seconds later, Kaleb strode back into the room, his erection now secured with latex as tight as a second skin.

As if by pure instinct, her legs spread apart, her painted toes going in two different directions in a silent invite to him and his dick—something she definitely thought needed a name of its own. Something mighty and strong like Thor . . . or Apollo.

Kaleb climbed between her legs, grabbing one around the ankle to raise it so that he could kiss her foot. Her ankle. Her calf. The soft skin behind her knee. And then her thigh.

He felt her body quiver. He raised his eyes to

look at her and reveled in the way her head was flung back, her eyes closed, and her mouth slightly parted as she panted a little.

On he went with his warm kisses and delicates licks. Farther up her thigh. To the top of the plump mound to suckle the tattoo that had teased and taunted during her strip show.

"Aah," she cried out weakly, grabbing her plush pillows with tight fists.

He licked around her belly button, enjoying the softness of her abdomen as he blew a stream of cool air against it.

"That feels sooooooo good," she said, biting her bottom lip.

And so he did it again.

"Mmmm." She squirmed. "I think you just discovered my hot spot."

And once more.

"Whoo."

He kissed a trail up to the valley of her breasts and suckled the warm spot as he stretched his body down over hers. His dick now pressed against the top of her left thigh, the hairs on his chest and his bronzed skin against her belly. He brought his hands up to grasp the sides of her breasts, bringing them in close together before he nuzzled his face against them and then captured one brown, taut nipple in his mouth.

Zaria grasped the back of his head, his soft silver hairs tickling against her palms as she arched her back off the bed. His tongue flickered around and against one nipple . . . and then the other . . . and then both.

"Shit," she swore, her clit jumping to renewed life.

Kaleb suckled her nipples deeper into his mouth, giving them all of his attention as he drew on the pleasure written all over her face and in the subtle changes to her body. He wanted to please her. He wanted to make sure that long after the night was over, she would never forget him and what he did to and for her. He wanted to make an impression. He wanted to set the bar high for anyone who dared come behind him.

Zaria pressed her hands against his shoulder, but she met resistance.

Kaleb lifted his head from her breast and looked up at her. "Just lie back and let me do this," he said deeply, then shifted up to settle his body on hers, his face directly above hers.

"I like to give as good as I get," she whispered.

Kaleb smiled as he lowered his head. "Next time," he promised.

Zaria wrapped her legs around his back. "Who says there will be a next time?" she asked saucily.

Kaleb captured her mouth in a kiss as he slid his hands beneath her body to cup her ass and lift her hips high, working his own hips to probe her open core with his thick tip. He broke the kiss just long enough to say, "I'll make sure of it right now."

And as he plunged his tongue into her mouth, Kaleb entered her swiftly.

Zaria's eyes widened at the hardness of him against her walls. "Wait, wait, wait," she begged, her heart pounding wildly in desire and a bit of fear. *Oh. My. God.*

Kaleb paused. Just a few inches of his dick was planted within her. The thick vein running along the length of him throbbed as rapidly as his heartbeat. He dropped his head to her shoulder, his breathing ragged as he fought for control. As he fought the primal urge to give in to the sweet goodness he found inside of her, wanting to fill her with every thick inch until no air could touch it.

"I'm sorry," he whispered against her neck. "Am I hurting you?"

Zaria kissed the hollow of his throat, tasting the saltiness of his sweat as she lightly dragged her fingertips from the top of his square buttocks up to the small of his back and then up to his broad shoulders.

"Your hands feels good," he admitted.

Zaria smiled before she kissed a path from the base of his neck to his shoulder. "Your dick feels good."

Kaleb turned his head and nuzzled her cheek. "You ready?" he asked thickly, hoping that she was. Wanting to feel more of her. The heat. The wetness. The tightness. All of it coupled with the energy between them was making him feel wild and hungry for her.

Zaria uncrossed her legs and opened them wide, causing her buttocks to shift a bit higher in the air and widening the opening to her core to him. For him. For *it.*

Kaleb kissed her, gently sucking her tongue and massaging the soft flesh of her buttocks to both please and distract her as he continued to enter slowly. And finally when he felt her adjust around him, accepting him, he entered her fully with one swift thrust.

Both of their bodies went still as they clutched each other tightly.

Zaria wrapped her ankles over the backs of his knees as she felt his hard heat pulsing inside of her. *Thump-thump. Thump-thump.*

"Don't move," he pleaded. "I don't want to come yet."

Zaria lightly bit his shoulder. "You better not. You talked way too much trash to go out this early."

Kaleb looked down at her. "Oh, you got jokes, huh?" he asked, liking that she was playful and sexy all at once—but there was a time to play and a time to get serious.

Kaleb grasped her waist and then sat back on his haunches, jerking her hips to pull her buttocks up onto the top of his upper thighs, her legs dangling over his bent arms. The move surprised her as she sat up with elbows pressed into her bed.

"Whoa," she said, looking at him like *What's coming next?*

Humph.

Kaleb lifted his buttocks off his haunches as he worked her hips and buttocks up and down, sending his dick against her clit and her G-spot with each rhythmic thrust inside her walls.

Zaria's eyes glazed over as she bit her bottom lip with a moan filled with every bit of pleasure she felt. "Oooooh my," she whispered, enjoying the feel of him as she watched the muscles of his chest, abs, arms, thighs, and buttocks flex with each slick and concentrated movement.

His eyes took in everything about her, missing nothing. The pleasure on her face. The fast beating of the pulse at the base of her throat as she let her head fall back. The way her hard brown nipples pointed toward the ceiling as the soft flesh of her breasts bounced up and down. The sight of his fingers digging into her hips. Her thick thighs spread wide. Her swollen clit, pink and glistening, freed from her brown hairless lips. The sight of his hard inches gliding in and out of her core.

"Damn, it's good," he moaned, closing his eyes as he let his own head fall back.

Sweat coated his body during the workout, but he was relentless, going from a slow and easy rocking motion to faster, quicker, and deeper thrusts filled with his strength and spurred on by her moans and purrs.

"Kaleb," she gasped.

His lips pursed at the feel of the spasms of her walls against his length as her core filled with a burst of heat and moisture. He knew she climaxing, and he looked down at her, his own face filling with a fierce determination.

"I'm coming," she gasped, her elbows collapsing from underneath her, causing her upper body to lightly flop down onto the bed.

Zaria felt a tiny explosion burst inside of her until she felt as if she were floating on air. He continued to pound her hips down onto his hardness, her buttocks lightly slapping against his upper thighs. Her loud and rough cries floated to the ceiling as she allowed her climax to control her. To free her. To complete her. "Yesssss," she cried out.

Her release pushed him over the edge into his own.

Kaleb stiffened as everything inside of him exploded. His movements became uneven as he fought for control as his release froze his body and made the tip of his member sensitive.

With a few final and hard thrusts, he grunted, completely spent.

Their panted breaths filled the air as their bodies went lax.

Kaleb freed his member and then shifted to sit on the edge of the bed, pressing his elbows against his knees as his head dropped to his chest. He felt completely exhausted and spent. He wanted nothing more than to climb into bed and sleep. And then he wanted to awaken and have more of her.

But it was her house . . . and her call.

Zaria swallowed a lump in her throat as she looked at him. She reached out with a still-shaky leg to nudge his back, already feeling sleep consume her.

Kaleb looked over at her with sleep in his own eyes.

"Come to bed, Kaleb," she said softly, wanting his hard and warm body beside her.

"Be right back," he said, rising to walk to her bathroom.

Moments later, her toilet flushed.

He walked back into the room, his body just as beautiful but his member now limp but still impressive, even at rest.

It took all her will to raise her arms—which felt like dead weights—to applaud him as he climbed into bed and pulled her body back against his with a chuckle.

Soon, both of their soft snores filled the air.

Late Saturday evening, Zaria stirred awake with a little moan. She frowned a little at the cool drool spot against her face. *Damn!* She wiped around her mouth as she sat up in the bed.

Kaleb stirred in his sleep with a little grunt before he went right back into a light snore. His body was sprawled out, one leg hanging off the bed and the rumpled sheet barely covering his stomach and privates.

Zaria smiled as she wiped her makeup-free face with her hands. She understood his fatigue. They hadn't left the house once. Just hours upon hours of leftovers, lounging, and lovemaking—or rather lustmaking, because Zaria wanted no part of any kind of love from a man.

She crept out of bed, leaving Kaleb reluctantly behind as he snorted and turned over onto his side, causing the sheet to fall and expose his caramel back and buttocks to her.

Kaleb was sleeping like an oversized baby, and this time *she* deserved the applause. During their last sexual escapade, she had taken the lead with a reverse cowgirl ride that left him literally begging her to stop.

Zaria did a little dance as she made her way to the bathroom to quickly brush her teeth, wash her face, and pull a ventilated brush through the tangled ends of her weave. She fought the urge to apply light makeup before lighthearted steps carried her out of the bathroom. She checked to make sure he was still hibernating and then danced her nude body into the living room to see if she had any messages on her answering machine.

She had turned off the ringer on her landline because she wanted *no* interruptions this weekend. She'd asked him to spend the weekend with her and he'd agreed. Chitchat with her daughters or her best friends—Chanci and Hope—would have to wait until she finally kissed him good-bye tomorrow.

Zaria fully intended to enjoy herself with Kaleb and their intense chemistry. Then she was going to send him and every inch of his skillful dick happily on his way and get back to enjoying the second half of her life—which was turning out to be way more fun than the first half. Way, way more.

"Good morning."

Zaria looked over her bare shoulder to find Kaleb leaning against the door frame of her bedroom. She licked her lips and allowed herself to take him all in. He had nothing to be ashamed of.

Even though she was proud of her own body, she still sucked her stomach in a bit before she turned to walk over to him. She loved how his dick hardened, lengthened, and rose from its resting position as he watched her like a hawk. "Why are you up?" Zaria asked as she neared him and wrapped a hand around his heated, rigid tool.

Kaleb's hips arched a bit as she massaged the length of him between their bodies. "I had a headache I thought you could help me with," Kaleb said, looking pointedly down at his erection.

"Oh, you did, huh?" she asked, stepping up beside him with his heat still firmly in her hand. She continued into the room, pulling him around and behind her, leading him by his maleness.

"I do," Kaleb answered thickly.

"Let's see what I can do."

"Yes, ma'am."

Early Sunday morning, Kaleb checked his missed calls on his cell phone as soon as he climbed inside his pickup truck. He called his foreman and let him know he wouldn't be on the farm until later that evening. The calls from his mother he ignored and called Kade instead as he steered his truck out of Zaria's yard.

"Whaddup, little brother?"

"Hey. Listen, I won't be home until later on tonight," Kaleb said as he pulled to a red light.

Kade laughed. "One of the exes actually worked out?" he asked in disbelief.

All of his brothers had advised him to leave his past in the past.

Kaleb shook his head as if his brother could see him thirty miles away in Holtsville. "No, I . . . uh . . . I met someone new," he admitted.

"On your date *with someone else*?" Kade asked.

"Kinda . . . but not really." Once the light turned green, Kaleb turned the truck into the parking lot of CVS. Summerville had more amenities and stores than Holtsville and was larger in size. The two cities were neighbors, but one was Mayberry and the other was a mini-New York in comparison.

"What happened?"

Kaleb parked in a spot near the front of the store as he gave Kade the rundown on getting walked out on by his date and then meeting Zaria. "She fine, too, Kade. She bad as hell."

"Get the hell outta here," Kade said. "Wait till I tell the brothers *this* shit, Mr. Ready to Settle Down."

Kaleb shut his truck off and climbed out. "No, I really do want to find Miss Right . . . but um . . . you know . . . I can still have fun until I do, right?"

"Oh, most definitely."

He squinted his deep-set eyes against the blazing summer sun. "Just run interference on Ma. You know how she get if she can't reach us—especially since I'm missing church."

"Got it."

All the brothers knew the drill. Their mother kept up with her children. Sometimes too much. They figured out that as long as one of the other siblings supplied some sort of detail on the whereabouts of the others, then she called off the dogs.

Kaleb flipped his phone closed as he walked into the pharmacy. He walked up to the counter. "Excuse me. Where are the condoms?" he asked the thin petite woman in the red uniform jacket.

"Aisle two," she said, eyeing him up and down

before she went back to stacking mini bottles of hand sanitizer by the register.

"Thanks." He patted the countertop before he headed toward the aisle. He grabbed a triple pack of ribbed Magnums, then thought twice about it and grabbed a twelve-pack instead. *Just in case,* he thought as he rushed around the store for deodorant and a toothbrush. Kaleb made his way back to the cashier.

She rang up the deodorant. And then the toothbrush. She pointedly eyed the box of condoms and then looked up at him. "Ooooh . . . not the twelve-pack," she muttered under her breath, her voice slightly squeaky.

Kaleb pressed one of his hands on the counter as he looked away from her and then back down at her, saying nothing.

"Excuuuuuse me, Mr. One in a Million, Hard to Believe, Who You Think You Fooling," she said, turning up her lips before she scooped up the box to scan.

What the hell? Kaleb eyed her. "Don't be jealous on your man's behalf," he said.

She looked comically aghast, pressing her hand to her chest and leaning farther back than Fat Joe. "Oh, I know you didn't!"

"Oh, yes, I did," he said, mocking her voice, facial expression, hand press to the chest, and lean.

Someone in line behind him giggled at the exchange.

Kaleb slid a crisp fifty-dollar bill across the counter before he turned. A little old lady in the biggest going-to-church hat he'd ever seen tilted her head back to wink at him mischievously.

"Ma'am," he said politely with a nod before grabbing his bag and change.

As he walked out of the store, he thought he heard her tell the cashier, "Whoever he headed to gonna need a *good* soak after it's all said and done."

Kaleb laughed as he pulled out his cell phone. He dialed the number Zaria gave him before he left her house. It rang twice.

"I'm on the way back. You need anything?" he asked, tossing the bag onto the seat.

"Just you . . . back in bed."

Kaleb's nature stirred.

"I'm lying in bed thinking of you and the things I would like to do to you," she said in a husky and soft voice meant to tease and tantalize.

"Oh yeah?" he said, starting the car and driving out of the parking lot . . . quickly.

"I thought I should wait for you, but then I thought why not get it ready for him. Set the scene. Stir up the mood. You know?"

Kaleb felt his manhood stiffen and slide down between his thigh and jeans as he envisioned her naked in bed with her hands pressed to places he wanted to touch himself.

She moaned into the phone softly. "It's funny, when I was a kid, I hated cats. Now here I am stroking a kitty."

He trembled. "Is it wet?" he asked thickly, shifting in the driver's seat as he drove as fast as safety and sanity allowed.

"Very," she said, then released a deep, purrlike sigh into the phone.

Kaleb spotted a police car parked up ahead on the side of the road and forced himself to ease off the gas pedal. The last thing he wanted was to get stopped by the police with a hard-on.

"Hmmm."

He looked into the rearview mirror, and as soon as he could no longer see the police cruiser, he gunned the gas. He stirred up dirt and pebbles turning into Zaria's dirt-packed front yard.

"This feels so good. Hurry, Kaleb, I need you inside me. Please hurry."

Kaleb put his phone on speaker and set it on the dash. "Get it ready for me," he told her as he rose off the seat to unzip his pants and free his erection. It felt like hard heat in his hands as he took one of the condoms from the box and unrolled it down the long, curving length.

"How do you want it, Kaleb? Where do you want it?"

"I want you on your back with your legs wide open waiting for me," he said, covering his erection with his shirt and the bag as he left the truck and jogged up the stairs to the front door with his phone in his hand.

"Hmmm. Come get it."

Kaleb paused with his hand on the doorknob at the visual. He felt weak in the knees and anxious through his whole body. "I'm coming," he told her, opening the door and closing his phone.

He strode quickly to the bedroom, the sounds of her moans echoing in the air and hurrying his strides. He paused at the doorway, taking in the sight of her body on the edge of the bed positioned and waiting just as he'd asked. Without saying a word, he let his jeans fall to the tops of his shoes as he walked up to stand before her, eased her moist fingers out of the way, and entered her with one deft thrust that caused them both to shudder and cry out.

Hours later, long after the sun had descended and their sexy seclusion drew to an end, both Kaleb and Zaria moved with slow reluctance. Their weekend was over.

Zaria stepped in front of the mirror over her dresser as she tightened the belt of her silk print robe and then twisted her hair into a loose knot at the base of her neck. Her eyes shifted to take in his reflection as he dressed by her bed.

"I know you're ready to change out of those clothes," she told him, turning to press her buttocks against the dresser as she watched him pull his beater T-shirt over his head and tuck it into his open denims.

Kaleb looked over at her. "It was worth it," he told her, sitting down on the bed to slide his shoes on.

In that moment, she felt like she could watch him forever. That didn't sit well with her. She was beyond the point in her life of being sprung. She'd made a decision to welcome him into her life for just the weekend. No relationships. No dates. No asking for more. It was what it was and it was over.

That weird vibe between them was all out of their systems.

She smiled a bit as he rose and walked over to stand in front of her. She took his hand and turned to lead him to the front door. She opened it wide and leaned back against it to look up at his handsome face.

Kaleb leaned down to lightly touch her side as he pressed a lingering kiss to her smooth cheek. "I'll call you sometime," he said. His words landed against her skin; then he turned and walked out the door.

Zaria was surprised at the sense of loss and regret she felt.

CHAPTER 5

From atop his favorite horse, Danger, Kaleb skillfully maneuvered the last of his cows into the paddock. Growing and maintaining lush pastures for the cows to graze all year long was a vital part of his farming. His cows needed great nutrition to produce milk, and waiting for green pastures just in the spring had been too risky.

After lots of research and attending lectures by successful dairy farmers, Kaleb focused his energy on ten different paddocks that he used to rotate the herds all year long. Increased natural nutrition for the cow increased his profits from the annual herd-milking average of twenty thousand pounds.

Of course, there was more to the farm, like disposing of the waste not used for fertilizer, keeping the milking facility clean, keeping bulls to breed the cows for calves, and much more. Kaleb had a full staff of twenty employees who were as equally loyal and hardworking as he was a well-paying, fair employer to them.

"Lordan, can you finish this up?" he called out to one of his ranch hands, a twenty-year-old who had been working with him every summer since he was fifteen. He'd hired him on full-time once he graduated high school two years ago.

"No problem, sir," Lordan called back from atop his horse.

Kaleb galloped across the flat plain toward the hub of his expansive farm. As he passed the milk parlor and then stopped in front of the metal stable, he saw in the distance that there was a car parked in front of his house, which was near the front of the property. He was too far away to recognize anything about it except its bright red color.

Dismounting, he handed the reins to one of the teenaged stable boys working for him. "Make sure to wipe him down and get him some water."

"Yes, sir."

He climbed onto his dusty Kawasaki Mule—a multipurpose vehicle that was like a combo of an ATV and a small pickup truck. Kaleb shooed away one of the stray dogs that had taken up residence on his ranch. He didn't have the heart to take them to the pound, so he made sure they were well fed and took them to Bianca's veterinary practice to have them checked, but he definitely wasn't looking for a pet—not like Kahron, who had his dog Hershey riding shotgun everywhere.

Kaleb checked the time on his cell phone. It was just after three. Usually he liked to pitch in right along with his staff, but he had some other business to tend to off the ranch. As he neared his house, he saw a woman on his porch. Her back was to him. She was tall and curvy with long straight hair.

His heart raced as he pulled to a stop by his pickup truck. *Zaria!*

She turned to face him, but he didn't recognize the woman. He couldn't deny the sharp disappointment he felt that it wasn't Zaria. Over the last week, memories of her had come to him at the oddest moments. Her smile. The brightness in her eyes when she laughed. The smell of her neck. The feel of her legs around his waist. The way she purred like a kitten and then roared like a lioness when she was climaxing. The steady pulse deep within her walls.

His nature stirred at the thought of her, but that and his excitement instantly deflated when the woman started speaking.

"Mr. Strong? Kaleb Strong?" she asked, giving him a smile.

Kaleb climbed out of the Mule. "Yes, ma'am," he said politely, adjusting his baseball cap lower over his eyes to block the sun. "Can I help you?"

"Aren't you the Southern gentleman?" she said teasingly with a false Southern accent as she leaned against the railing of his porch.

Kaleb eyed her as he climbed the stairs slowly. She was tall and curvy with a cute round face and a pouty mouth. "I try," he said with a smile.

She continued to stare at him.

Kaleb began to feel awkward as he reached the

top step. "Ma'am, can I help you with something?" he asked again.

"Actually, I'm Ellie Hunt. I'm an insurance agent. Your mother thought you might need some additional policies for yourself or any of your properties," she said, extending her arm with a business card in her hand.

Kaleb hid his face as he looked down at the card. The last thing he needed was more insurance. As his primary benefactor, his mother was well aware of that fact. Sending Miss Ellie to his home was pure matchmaking. And if his mom had given her the thumbs-up, he was sure Ellie was a single, churchgoing woman with no children and lots of manners.

Kaleb held her card out to her with a shake of his head. "Miss Hunt—"

"Ellie," she offered.

"Ellie, I have all the coverage I need," he said. "To be honest, ma'am, I hope I can avoid the whole sales pitch because I have an appointment—"

"No problem at all," she said, nodding in what he thought was understanding. "Let's quickly set up a time for me to come back and discuss some alternative policies."

Kaleb began to inch his body toward his solid black front door as she continued her sales pitch. "Ma'am," he began, any interest in asking her out ending. His hand was already surrounding the cool metal of the doorknob and turning it slowly.

"Yes, I'm sorry. I'm just running my mouth," she said, digging into the briefcase she held to pull out a handful of brochures. "I'm just compassionate about life and making sure the needs of you and your family are protected through adequate coverage. We can even review your current policy and compare it—"

Kaleb had opened the door and stepped inside his home, the cool rush of the central air-conditioning pressing up against the back of his body. "You have a good day, ma'am."

Her face shaped into a look of surprise as the door began to close and block her—and her sales pitch—from his view. "But—"

CLICK.

Kaleb wiped his eyes as he walked away from the door and deeper into the spacious open layout of his home. He didn't mean to be rude, but Miss Ellie the Insurance Lady didn't know how to take no for an answer. He understood she had a job to do, but she had ignored that he politely informed her he had another appointment. That same relentless nature might just translate into how she acted in relationships—Kaleb wasn't willing to risk it.

He frowned a bit as he looked around. *Damn.* He really needed to clean up. With the entire front portion of the house being one room, he felt that, as a large man, he wasn't confined by rooms and walls, but it also meant that his lack of consistent cleaning was glaringly displayed. Dirty dishes, old takeout containers, and random mail littered the low-slung wooden coffee table. His kitchen was in need of some serious elbow grease. Laundry needed to be washed—and some just needed to be folded and put away.

Seven years ago, the Jamison twins had built

his home to his specifications. The women in his family called it the ultimate bachelor pad. His walls were bare. His tables were free of accessories. There was a fine layer of dust everywhere. All of the furniture was chocolate leather—comfortable and functional.

With the right woman's touch, Kaleb knew his home could be a real showplace. The light streaming in through the dozens of floor-to-ceiling windows on the far ends of the house was meant to highlight beauty and not man clutter.

Releasing a heavy breath filled with the fatigue of a hard day's work, Kaleb blocked out the clutter and made his way across the wide expanse and down the hall running across the length of the home and separating the three large bedroom suites from the rest of the house—each equipped with its own bathroom and sitting room.

It was a home for a family.

Kaleb began to strip off his dusty clothes, leaving a trail on the floor behind him as he made his way into his master suite. Again chaos reigned. It was as if his clothes had been shoved into a cannon and then shot up into the air to explode in odd places around the room. *No time for that now.*

He rushed through a steaming hot shower and was just wrapping a towel around his waist when he heard voices from the outer area of his house. Frowning, he held the ends of the towel together with one strong hand as he made his way out of the bedroom. Feminine laughter filled the air. His eyebrows joined his mouth and deepened downward. *No, that heifer did not walk into my house,* he thought, expecting to find the Insurance Lady.

What the hell . . .

His step halted at the sight of three twenty-something ladies all looking at him, their mouths open.

"Surprise, surprise," one of them said with a tiny bite of her bottom lip as her eyes locked on his imprint against the towel.

"Hey, Big Bubba, you're home," his sister Kaitlyn called from the spacious kitchen area.

Eyeing the whispering, ogling, and pointing women warily, Kaleb backed into his room. "Excuse me," he said.

One of the women let out a girlish catcall just as he closed the door securely. He was happy to see his wild, always-on-the-move sister, but a call—or at least a ring of the doorbell—would be great first. Curious about her sudden reappearance, he rushed into boxers and sweatpants and a V-neck T-shirt. Barefoot, he padded back out into the house and found Kaitlyn and her crew now in his kitchen.

Kaitlyn turned, her once-long and flowing thick hair now a jet-black pixie cut that framed her slender face and emphasized the bright eyes she inherited from their mother. Her slender frame was in a strapless jumpsuit that he knew cost his father a small fortune. Kaitlyn was the baby of the Strong clan and the only girl. Her wish was their father's command. She had the old man snuggled into the palm of her hand. She was the princess diva of their family.

"Hi, Kaleb," the ladies all said in sweet unison and they waved their manicured fingertips at him.

"Cool down, girls," Kaitlyn said, moving her five-foot-ten-inch frame forward to wrap her arm around his strong neck. "This is one of my big brothers and not one of those Brazilian lover boys we left on the beaches."

Kaleb frowned. "That's more than I need to know," he drawled, kissing her cheek before moving around the stone island to grab a personal-sized juice from his double fridge.

"Well, we just got back from Brazil, and I had to use the bathroom and you know I don't do public restrooms . . . although yours wasn't much better," Kaitlyn said with a dismissive wave of her hand. She eased her body up onto the edge of the island and lightly kicked her feet back and forth like she didn't have a care in the world.

That's because she didn't. Kaleb actually thought his parents and their oldest brother Kade weren't doing Kaitlyn any favors by spoiling her. She'd never had a job, she didn't take college seriously before she dropped out, and she knew absolutely nothing about the family business—or any other business for that matter.

Except shopping and going on vacations.

"You could help your brother out and handle it," he joked, pointedly ignoring the way her friends eyed him as if he were raw flesh to a pack of werewolves.

All of their faces shaped into looks of horror and shock.

Kaleb just laughed. "Well, I have plans, so

if you and the pretty committee are through visiting . . ."

Kaitlyn's friend waved at him as they made their way to the front door on gold high heels that reminded him of Zaria. And that made him think of Zaria. And made him want to see Zaria. And have Zaria. Be in Zaria.

But his life was about settling down and starting a family. . . .

As amazing as their chemistry had been and probably still was, as much as he still thought of her, as deeply as he found himself missing her, Kaleb honestly didn't know if he was comfortable settling down with a woman who was willing to have a fling weekend. And if she was having this carefree lifestyle of clubbing and having flings, was settling down remotely on her list of things to do?

Of course, he had the fling as well, but even in 2011 the standards for a man and his sexuality were lower than those for women—especially in the South. His mama had taught their sister early that a man could sleep with a hundred women and be called a playboy. A woman dared to have a hundred known lovers and she was called a whore. To add insult to injury, that label would stick with that woman forever—even if she settled down and remained faithful to one man. Then the whispers would be, "Whooo-wee she used to be a ho back in her day."

He thought of the reaction of his father and brothers at the news of his friend marrying a woman with a "reputation." They instantly thought he was a fool looking for trouble and headed for a life of men slipping in and out through the back door of his home while he was away.

Things were just different for men and women. Right, wrong, or indifferent. *It is what it is.*

He had doubts about anything more than a casual "see you when I see you" relationship with Zaria.

Still, he couldn't stop thinking of her. It had been a very long time since a woman had claimed such a big part of focus. A very long time.

"Anyway, Big Bubba Number Three, your baby sister saw the cutest shoes at the mall, but I'm a little strapped for cash with my little vacay and all," she said, giving him that smile she'd used on all of them since she was big enough to toddle.

Had to use the bathroom my ass. Kaleb walked back to his bedroom to swoop up the dirty pants he'd worn that day. He grabbed his wallet and headed back out of the bedroom. "You need to fill out an application at all those stores where you shop," he said, pulling two crisp fifty-dollar bills from the wads snuggled there.

Kaityln looked down into the wallet, took the hundred dollars he gave her, and pulled out a hundred more—with that smile. "Thanks, Bubba," she said sweetly with an exaggerated Southern accent that was so fake but so adorable.

"All you need is the right man with the balls and backbone to straighten you out, Kat," he called behind her.

She stopped and looked at him with her shaped eyebrow arched and a twinkle in her eye. "That man doesn't exist because I always get what I want," she said, shaking the crisp bills at him before she blew him a kiss and walked out the door.

By the time she hit up every member of the family, his sister would have well over a grand or better to blow at the mall. He just shook his head because he helped spoil her just like all the other Strong men, and that spelled trouble for a man fool enough to try and tame her.

Zaria poured herself a glass of her favorite brand of Moscato before she danced her way to the living room as Kanye West and Jay-Z's duet "H.A.M." blared through the surround-sound system. Dressed in a thong and an oversized striped men's dress shirt, she paused long enough to do an old-school wop before settling down in the corner of the chair and then tucking her feet beneath her.

It was midnight. Her feet hurt from working in heels all night, and she didn't feel like going to sleep. In fact, this last week, sleep had become its own kind of hell for her. In her slumber, she had no control of the content of her dreams. There were no distractions . . . from memories and re-creations of her time with Kaleb.

"Ugh!" she growled, lightly pounding her fist against her bare thigh as she shook her head to free the image of him—sexy and silver and strong.

She didn't want to be caught up . . . or be in a relationship.

During the weekend together, they had shared explosive sex, but there was also something about him that made her feel secure and comfortable.

It was those feelings—plus that damned vibe—that led her to invite a complete stranger into her home and her bed after just a few hours of dancing together closely in a club.

Her first one-night—or one-weekend—stand.

Zaria pretended she didn't feel her neck and cheeks fill with warmth as she focused on the music and her wine. *"I'm about to go H.A.M. Hard as a motha—"*

Bzzzzzz . . . bzzzzzz . . . bzzzzzz . . .

She set her goblet on the low-slung coffee table as she picked up her vibrating cell phone. She used the remote to mute the volume on the sound system and flipped the phone open. "Hello, ladies," she said, knowing that although Hope's number was on the caller ID both of her friends were on the line.

"Hey, girl."

"Hello, hello, hello."

"It took y'all long enough to call me back," Zaria said.

"But we did call back, so what's the nine-one-one?" Hope asked.

"I met a cute guy last weekend—"

"What else is new?" Chanci interrupted.

Zaria shifted her eyes heavenward. "We spent the whole weekend together," she admitted.

"Huh?" one of them said.

"I met a guy. We clicked. I mean we *really* clicked, and I brought him home for the weekend." Zaria winced as she waited for her friends' reactions.

"Z, I know damn well you did not invite a stranger into your house!" Chanci squealed.

"O-*kay,*" Hope chimed in. "What if he was a rapist?"

"Or a murderer?"

"What were you thinking?"

"Yes, what in the hell were you thinking, Z?"

Zaria rubbed her hand over her eyes. "It was dumb and I was blessed that he wasn't those things. I won't ever do it again. Are we all done?" she asked. "Can I get to my real problem?"

"Being chopped into a million pieces and being made into stew ain't a problem?" Hope snapped.

"I couldn't exactly be on the phone with you heifers if I was in a pot of Zaria stew right now. Mo-ving on."

They both sighed.

Zaria closed her eyes as she weaved her fingers through her hair. She thought of Kaleb. "Great googa-mooga, he was fine," she said, envisioning the first moment she looked up at him in the crowded foyer of the restaurant.

"Tall and muscular and handsome with silver hair—"

"Silver? You talking about an older dude?" Hope asked. "You?"

"He's prematurely gray and it works for him. Believe me. It works. It just really works."

"We got it. It works," Chanci teased dryly.

They all laughed.

Zaria lay back against the chair as she fanned between her thighs playfully. "I will spare you the intimate details, but the man is built to please," she said. "Over and over and over again."

Chanci hummed approvingly. "He sounds like my man."

"Mine, too, baby," Hope said.

Zaria could clearly hear the happiness of her formerly lovelorn sistahs. They both were in fulfilling and committed relationships, and although it wasn't her thing, she honestly was happy for them. "That reminds me," she began, sitting up to retrieve her wine goblet for a deep sip of the sparkling sweet wine.

They both remained silent.

"I'm waiting on you both to tell me I was right."

"For?" Hope asked.

"Yes, do tell," Chanci added, sounding amused.

Zaria smoothed her jet-black hair back behind her softly rounded shoulders. "I been schooling you horny heifers on the wonders of a younger man way before your young bucks got your noses—*and* your legs—wide open."

"Ozi's not exactly a young man," Hope insisted, even though the truth was in her crisp tones.

"But he's younger than you," Zaria countered, stretching out to lie on the sofa and cross her legs at her shapely ankles. "And, Chanci, your little roughneck probably wears his Timbs when you do the do, right? And you like it . . . don't you?"

The laughter that bubbled out of Chanci's throat was all too telling.

"Yes, but what you told us about had everything to do with sex—"

"And nothing to do with love," Chanci finished in pure satisfaction.

"Well, I'm not looking for love," Zaria said with honesty, her eyes seeking and finding the now-empty spot over the fireplace where her wedding photo had sat for her entire marriage. "Been there. Done that. Got screwed—and not in a good way."

"There's more to life than nine inches, Zaria," Hope admonished, easily slipping into mother mode.

Zaria imagined Kaleb naked, hard, and ready. "You're right. There's ten," she said decidedly. "*Even* eleven."

"Okay, so you ran into a sexy young guy with a big woo-woo. What's the nine-one-one?" Chanci asked, sounding like she was chewing on ice.

"I can't get him off my mind. I think about him a lot. And that's not what I want."

"We all know you got what you wanted," Hope said dryly.

Zaria closed her eyes and rested her forearm against the closed lids. "And I want more. Lots more. And not just the incredible sex . . . but the laughing and joking, and the way he likes to hold me after sex and rub my lower back, and the way he likes to kiss, and his smell. I want more of it all. All of it."

"So call him, Z."

Zaria shook her head as she wiggled her toes. "He's too addictive. He is too necessary. He is . . . is like drugs. I just have to say no or I'll be 'round here shaking and shit. Out in the middle of the night with a damn dick radar and a flashlight looking for it, you know?"

"So don't call him."

Zaria kicked her feet up in the air, silently wishing she could plant one of them dead in the center of Chanci's behind. "I haven't called him. I'm not going to. I just need to get him off my mind—and out my dreams and out of my system."

"That sounds like a plan."

"Or . . . ," Hope added.

Zaria arched a brow. "Or what?"

"*Or* . . . maybe you can see how good it is to be in a relationship with someone."

Zaria shivered in mock horror. "No," she stated firmly.

Their story was not hers and hers was not theirs. She understood that maybe they didn't completely understand where she was coming from. That was cool. They were the best of friends but they didn't share one brain and thus one thought. No one else could walk a mile in her stilettos.

"I wasted so many good years of my life on the ex, and I just want to get to know me and enjoy it, you know," she admitted, looking up at the slowly turning ceiling fan. "My divorce and everything about it really messed me up, and I'm just trying to enjoy relying on me, and enjoying me, and discovering things that I missed while playing Suzie Homemaker while my husband was out screwing another woman."

"Oh, Zaria." One of them sighed sadly.

She hated their pity but she understood because it *was* damn pitiful. "I just want to have fun," she stressed.

"Well looky here, Cyndi Lauper," Chanci drawled. "Maybe all the fun you're looking for is right there with that younger man."

Hope chuckled. "Just lay your cards on the table and let him know you have an itch you want scratched every now and then and nothing more, and if he's willing, then *enjoy* it, Z."

Zaria bit the side of her thumbnail. She had dated a lot of younger men since her divorce, but the numbers she allowed into her bed had been very few. Still, she enjoyed the way they were so eager to please her, and the idea of seeing Kaleb again sent excited shivers down her spine. There was a comfortable nature and an explosive chemistry between them that scared her.

She couldn't give in to the yearning. She knew deep in her gut, with every fiber of the women's intuition she ignored in the past, that Kaleb Strong was not an easy man to get over. She absolutely could not take the risk.

Kaleb couldn't sleep. For the past hour, he had tossed and turned and then flipped and flopped all over his bed. His sheets and covers were in total disarray around his legs. He reached down and picked up his cell phone lying against the stark whiteness of his sheet in the darkness. He flipped it open and scrolled through his list of contacts. The numbers of many women—past and present—were stored, but his eyes searched for just one.

"Zaria." He read her highlighted name softly,

his calloused thumb lightly brushing against the CALL button.

He wanted to call her and hear her voice. See how she was doing. Inquire about her week. Tell her that he couldn't stop thinking of her.

But why start something they couldn't finish?

He flipped his phone closed, and it instantly began to vibrate in his hand. His gut clenched to see Zaria's number. Without hesitation, he flipped it open, his heart hammering. "Hello."

Kaleb heard nothing but the dial tone.

Sitting up in the middle of his bed, he called her back.

Zaria jumped as her cell phone vibrated. She eyed her phone sitting on the coffee table. She picked it up, knowing it was Kaleb.

Crossing her legs on the couch, she turned the television down and answered her phone, feeling an odd mix of sickness and excitement. *Get it together, Zaria.*

"I didn't hang up quick enough, huh?" she asked, feeling more than a little embarrassed to be caught changing her mind about contacting him.

"So you didn't mean to call me?" he asked.

She laughed a little as she played with the edges of her shirt like a nervous schoolgirl. "I thought maybe you could come over," she admitted, her voice and body a bundle of nerves.

He paused. "I wish I could, but it's so late and I have to get up at three to work my farm."

Zaria felt her disappointment intensely. "Oh . . .

okay . . . well, I guess I'll speak to you whenever, then," she said softly. "And we'll do whatever then too."

Kaleb laughed low in his throat. "I guess so," he agreed.

Zaria felt like doing a childish pout. She wasn't used to these young men turning her down. *Bad enough I had to call him and now this? Oh, hell to the no . . .*

"Your loss," she said, trying to be flippant.

"So we can't talk?" he asked. "It's just dick or nothing? Damn."

That surprised—and pleased—her. "Talk about what?"

"Anything. Everything. Tell me about yourself," he encouraged. "There's more to you than the physical, right?"

She stood up, her shirt falling down around her bottom as she walked over to the window to look out at the full moon. It glowed. But in that moment, as he gently nudged bits of her life from her, Zaria was sure the moon's radiance dimmed in comparison to her.

Chapter 6

Kaleb stirred in his sleep and was momentarily surprised by the feel of soft and warm breasts pressed against his back and a supple foot gently covering his. His body relaxed as he remembered that he was at Zaria's and that they both had fallen into a deep sleep after yet another round of explosive sex that was beyond addictive.

A smile spread across his face in the darkness as he remembered how Zaria's touch had brought him back to a full, steely hardness after he had just filled her with an explosive climax ten minutes earlier. He couldn't get enough of her. He didn't want to.

Over the last two weeks, Kaleb and Zaria had spent the weekdays talking by phone, and during the weekends they spent the entire forty-eight hours locked in Zaria's home, completely caught up in a passion neither could deny. If not for his workdays on his ranch beginning early and ending late, Kaleb knew he would make the forty-five-minute drive to Summerville to see her during the week.

Zaria shifted in her sleep, and just the movement of her foot up and down his calf caused goose bumps to race over his body. The simplest touch from her made his heart race. He was no newbie to the wiles of a woman—far from it—but something about Zaria made everything feel new and exciting again.

He reached for her hand lightly resting on his hip and slid it down to wrap her fingers and palm around his growing erection. And when her hand took the lead, gaining strength as sleep left her, Kaleb arched his hips forward, filling her hand with a thrust.

Soft lips pressed kisses to his back, from shoulder to shoulder, with a soft purr. She grasped the base of his dick firmly before easing her hand up and down the full length of him from his swollen and smooth tip and back down. Back and forth with just the right amount of pressure at the tip. He felt his slight release and she used that to lubricate the movement.

"Damn," he swore.

Zaria smiled against his back. Being awakened from her sleep with the feel of Kaleb's rod in her hand was a delight. A delicious one. She continued to massage him, enjoying the feel of his bare and hard buttocks against her fleshy mound as she cupped his body from behind with her own.

The last two weekends had been like a dream. They laughed. They joked. They ate. They made love. He was attentive. Respectful. Thoughtful. Fulfilling.

She was enjoying the ride. Loving every moment

of exploring his body and finding out what turned him on. She had discovered many, many things.

"Turn the lights on," she whispered into the darkness, reaching down to lightly drag her finger across his sac.

Kaleb leaned forward and touched the base of the lamp, softly illuminating the room.

"Turn over," she requested, already moving back to make room on the bed for his big and strong body, because she knew that he wouldn't deny her.

As soon as his back pressed down into the bed, she shifted to her knees, her buttocks high in the air as she bent down to circle his nipple with her tongue. He moaned. She suckled the tiny bud between pursed lips, the soft silver hairs of his chest tickling her mouth as she did.

"My dick got harder," he whispered to her, reaching up to push the dark sheet of her hair behind her ear.

Zaria cut her eyes up at him as she grasped his hardness with her hand again while she circled his dark bud as he lightly cupped the back of her thigh. "Touch me," she whispered hotly, lifting her buttocks higher and leaning her body over to suckle his other bud.

The first feel of his thick fingers reaching behind her to play in her moist flesh caused her to gasp and arch her back. She pressed the side of her face against his chest, the soft hairs cushioning her against the hardness of his biceps. She spread her knees, lowering her buttocks as he eased his fingers inside her, circling her walls, teasing her swollen clit, pressing the thick lips of her pussy.

Zaria cried out as his fingers began a rapid in-and-out motion. He bit his bottom lip and locked his hooded eyes on to her face. She knew he enjoyed seeing the pleasure he gave.

He reveled in her rapture.

She felt the same.

Zaria fought the urge to take his hardness into her mouth to suckle. *Not yet. It's too soon,* she thought, even as she craved the taste of him against her tongue.

Instead, she stroked him, being sure to squeeze and tease the tip just the way he liked as she placed kisses on his entire chest with details to his nipples. Each touch, stroke, kiss, and nibble made his body shiver beneath her.

"You wanna come now or later?" he asked thickly.

"Both," she said, before doing a snakelike motion with the tip of her tongue.

Kaleb's eyes watched the move, and he had to take his free hand from her hair to keep from guiding her head down until her tongue teased the tip of his dick. He couldn't deny that he wanted the treat from her, but it was a move he rarely requested, never wanting to offend. *Still . . .*

"Sit on my face," he said.

Zaria looked up at him, and he loved the way her eyes glazed over as she did as requested. As soon as her intimacy spread in front of him like a blooming flower, he sucked the whole of her sweetness into his mouth and then kissed each cheek of her smooth brown buttocks before burying his face between them and letting his tongue get lost inside her walls.

Zaria closed her eyes tightly as her back arched into a semicircle. She reached out to grab his ankles, forcing herself not to move as he devoured her with passion and promise. She just wanted to enjoy the work of a master, and he needed no help at all.

His erection grazed the side of her face. The scent of his body intrigued her. The thrill of exciting him taunted her.

With one deep breath, she turned her head and quickly took the tip of him into her mouth. He cried out against her core as she circled the smoothness with her tongue. She moaned deeply in pleasure and just enjoyed the taste of him. The strength. The smoothness. The hardness. All at once. Everything.

As he returned to pleasing her, Zaria pleased him as well.

They moved in perfect unison.

Soon, an energy she was now familiar with began with the tingling of her toes and up to the roots of her hair, feeling alive. With deep guttural gasps, her fingernails dug into his ankles as she climaxed again and again.

Kaleb grabbed her buttocks deeply at the first feel of her explosion against his tongue. He was thirsty for her juices and drank every drop, but as he felt his own climax building and finally exploding, he was sure he would lose his voice from roaring in fiery release like nothing he had ever known.

* * *

Hours later, Zaria was sitting on her front porch and sipping on a cup of brewed tea with lemon and honey. The sun was just beginning to rise beyond the towering trees, and the sound of nature was echoing in the air. Dressed only in Kaleb's oversized T-shirt, she swung back and forth on the swing her daughters had cherished while growing up. It was one of the few routines of her past that she hadn't relinquished. It had been many days that a quiet moment alone in their swing had brought her peace.

She had just needed a little breather from the sex marathon she and Kaleb were on. She had just wanted to enjoy seeing the sun rise alone.

Zaria hadn't expected to see her ex-husband's navy blue pickup truck pulling out of her backyard.

"What the hell?" she said, jumping to her bare feet and moving to the top of the step.

He pulled the truck to a stop in front of the house and lowered the passenger window. "I just came for my table saw," he said, leaning over to look at her out the open window.

Zaria's eyes took in the saw in the bed before shifting back to him. "You need to call and get my permission before you take things off my property, Ned," she said. "As a matter of fact, why don't you take out anything else you have stored in that shed so you have no reason to leave Boomqueisha home alone. The authorities don't like minors being left unsupervised."

Ned shook his round head. "I came for my saw and not your nickel on my wife."

Zaria leaned down and squinted her eyes before arching one brow and coming down the stairs with her mouth wide open. "Oh my God, Ned. Have you *dyed* your hair?" she shrieked, before throwing her head back to laugh.

"Jealousy doesn't look good on you, Zaria," he said, reaching for the baseball cap swinging from the rearview mirror and sliding it onto his head.

"And all that crispy jet-black hair looks crazy on you," she countered, pressing her bare feet into the dew-moistened grass to stand by the truck. "You wait until your behind is damn near dying for real to dye your hair. Bonita Applebaum got you messed up, playa."

He eyed her. "And what's the difference between that and all that fake hair glued to your head."

"I'm not as old as you?" she spouted.

"But you ain't as young as you think either."

"Humph, I'm old enough to drink, Cradle Robber."

"Maybe too old to drink, Grandma."

Zaria's mouth fell open. "No, you didn't."

Ned blew his horn twice before he pulled away.

She fought the childish urge to pick up a pebble and throw it like a pitcher in the Major League. Sipping from her tea, she turned and jogged up the stairs. She and Ned hadn't shared a kind word since their divorce.

Back when Meena and Neema were school-aged, she would have never imagined that her marriage would end. She had been it for the long haul. Through good, bad, and indifferent.

She knew now what she didn't know then. Their marriage had been comfortable. Routine. Ordinary. But there had been no passion for a long time. The sex was perfunctory before becoming damn near nonexistent. Their kisses were more out of habit than true intimacy. Their touches were that of strangers.

Did Ned find passion with his new wife? Had that been the reason he threw away their marriage? Had she been the one to give him the spark that faded from their marriage? Had something in Zaria pushed him to look for that energy?

She found it with Kaleb, but if Ned had never left her, she would have never strayed to find it. She had settled in with her husband for the long haul. Till death.

"Breakfast is ready."

Zaria looked up to find Kaleb standing in the open doorway. He wore nothing but his low-slung jeans and one of her aprons around his waist. She smiled at him, pushing away any thoughts of her failed marriage. "You cooked for me?" she asked.

Kaleb smiled. "I did my best anyway."

She walked past him into the house, fighting the urge to stop and taste his lips. She frowned a bit at the acrid smell of something burned.

"Ignore the smell. It's not as bad as it seems," he said with a chuckle from behind her.

Zaria smiled at him over her shoulder, thinking

she had never seen a more handsome chef. "It's the thought that counts," she said.

Zaria hated that her interaction with Ned had put a damper on her spirits, especially when she spotted the bacon, eggs, and waffles Kaleb cooked for them. "You've been busy," she said, taking the plate he handed her and sitting at the table that was covered in the sunlight.

"I was hungry and you looked like you were enjoying your tea and the swing," he said, taking a seat across from her at the table. "Until you were interrupted."

She looked at him as he cut his intense eyes over at her. "You saw that?"

He nodded and shrugged. "I heard a little bit too," Kaleb admitted. "I opened the window earlier to let the smoke out. I closed it once you two starting the verbal sparring."

"My ex makes my ass itch," she admitted around a bite of eggs.

Kaleb laughed.

Zaria looked up at him. "No, seriously," she said, her expression deadpan.

Kaleb's smiled faded a bit. "You want to tell me about it?" he asked, reaching across the table to stroke her face.

Zaria allowed herself to press her face against his warm palm even as she shook her head.

The simple gesture of kindness and concern nearly made the dam inside of her break, but she refused to let one tear fall, so she closed her eyes, breathed deeply, and got lost in the scent of

Kaleb's cologne. She hated that the pain of her divorce still surfaced so often.

"You'll have to let me show you my ranch."

Zaria allowed herself one more deep breath before opening her eyes to look at him. She smiled warmly. "Me and my stilettos on a ranch?" she quipped.

Kaleb gave her cheek one final stroke as he nodded. "Yeah, I want you to go horseback riding with me," he offered, picking up a very crispy strip of bacon.

Zaria raised a brow. "I'm a Southern girl for sure, but the only horse I've seen is Mr. Ed, sugar."

"Who?" he asked.

Zaria rolled her eyes heavenward at the twenty-something not knowing about the popular 1960s sitcom about a talking horse. "Never mind," she told him. "But that's a no on the horses. The only stallion I want to ride has two legs . . . not four."

Kaleb just shook his head at her.

He said nothing else about it, but Zaria had the feeling that she had disappointed him.

Still, me on a ranch?

Nearly two weeks later, Kaleb jogged up the steps of Zaria's porch, careful not to slip as droplets of the earlier rain remained. He straightened the tailored navy blue blazer he wore over a crisp white shirt and distressed jeans. He straightened his shoulders and took a breath just before he rang the bell. It seemed like more than two weeks since their last weekend shared together.

Zaria had had to work the past two weekends, and Kaleb had busied himself with the farm and his family.

After weeks of calling each other and continuing to get to know each other, he was looking forward to spending a night away from his busy farm and in the company of a woman. But not just any woman. Zaria.

And unlike their usual weekend rendezvous indoors, he had insisted that they leave the house and take a small break from constant sex. He had to see if there was more than the physical between them.

The door opened and he gave himself one last straighten of his blazer sleeves. He looked up from arranging his stainless-steel black-faced watch, his eyes widening in surprise.

Zaria wore a skintight fuchsia strapless dress that did little to hide that she was braless—and that the cool weather had hardened her nipples. As his eyes skimmed down her body, he thought he saw the slight indent of her G-string against her hip.

The outfit was bold. Sexy. Daring.

And completely inappropriate.

And too much.

Zaria smiled at him as she leaned over to pick up an oversized gold bag with lots of brassy buckles. "You look good, Kaleb," she said, stepping outside and closing the front door behind herself.

He stalled, placing a hand to her lower back as he leaned to kiss her cheek. "Um . . . you look good too," he said, deciding against asking her to change into something a little less in-your-face.

"I bought this today and couldn't wait to show it off to you," she said, slowly turning to model the dress for him.

There was no doubt she had the curvaceous hourglass shape that epitomized the healthy figure men loved about a black woman. And he enjoyed the sight of her firm buttocks and full breasts outlined against the spandexlike material. But damn . . .

Kaleb wiped his mouth, fighting the urge to at least convince her to grab a shawl. Zaria was a grown woman—and not even officially his woman. He knew he had no right to guide her choices.

"I think I might be getting a little attached to having you here," she said as they descended the stairs, his hand lightly at the small of her back.

"I'm looking forward to seeing you outside this house," he said, stepping forward to open the car door for her. "Let's see just what this thing is between us."

"But we know what it is," Zaria said.

"We do?"

Zaria cut her eyes up at him and pressed her hand to his chest. "Chemistry," she said.

Kaleb locked his eyes on her glossy mouth and then her eyes. That familiar current was palpable between them. "Chemistry," he repeated.

He was a man who paid attention to women. Their likes and dislikes. Their wants and desires. Their actions and reactions. As he stood there looking down at Zaria's eyes, he knew she wanted him. He knew he could say to hell with dinner and have her in bed. But he wanted to know there was more available from her than just sex.

He lowered his head as he cupped her face. The feel of her lips was like water quenching thirst. He vaguely wished the gloss wasn't in such abundance, but the feel of her tongue stroking his mouth was his total undoing. With a moan deep in his soul, he turned her body and shifted her around until she was pressed against the rear door of the SUV he rarely drove. His hands moved down to her waist and even farther down to her thigh to grab the hem of her dress and jerk it up roughly.

Zaria gasped, breaking their kiss as she tilted her head back and exposed her neck.

The sound of her sighs was fuel to his desire. Kaleb bent his knees to lightly flick his tongue against the base of her neck before he licked a slow and sensual trail up to her chin. He retraced the heated path as he grasped the top of her dress and snatched it down to her waist. The last rays of light from the fading sun highlighted the brown tips of her hard nipples as he dipped his silver-flecked head to take one deeply into his mouth. The feel of her body's shiver against his sent blood rushing to his loins until he was hard and long and ready.

"I have a helluva grill and a couple of rib eye steaks in the freezer," she whispered into the night summer air as she rubbed both of her hands against the back of his head.

Kaleb paused, his mouth still pressed to a soft breast as his mind worked quickly.

Is sex all she wants from me?

It is *good sex, though.*

But I'm looking for a wife, not a lover.

But it is *good sex.*

He thought of how he'd invited her to his farm and how she'd brushed the invite off like dust on her shoulder. His farm was a part of him—an important part—and she had no interest in it. Kaleb backed away, standing up to his full height, holding up his hands as if he were being stopped by the police. "Whooooo," he said, like he was trying to release pressure through a valve. "I can't think straight around you, Zaria."

She pulled her top back up to cover her breasts. "Looks like your mind's not the only thing that's not straight," she said, looking pointedly at his erection pressing against his zipper.

Kaleb dropped his hands to try and cover himself. "So I'm wrong to want to get to know you better?"

"And we can't do that here?" she asked, waving her hand back at her home, then using her fingertips to wipe away the remnants of lip gloss smeared around her mouth.

"So you don't want to go to dinner?" he asked.

"I was hoping everything this dress is saying would make you forget about dinner." Zaria turned, making sure to emphasize her jiggle and wiggle.

Kaleb felt his dick harden in a rush, and it lightly brushed against the palm of his hand as it grew.

"Let me cook dinner for you, Kaleb," she said simply.

"Just dinner?" he said, hating that he sounded wary and afraid of being alone with her.

"And dessert . . . maybe something with cherries," she said, already turning to walk back up the stairs to her house.

Kaleb slid his hands into her pockets as he watched the up and down movement of her buttocks in her dress. Zaria unlocked the front door and stood just long enough in the doorway to crook her finger to beckon him.

His intention tonight was to see if there could be more between them than just great sexual chemistry. He had been looking forward to taking her to one of his favorite downtown Charleston restaurants, but with her racy outfit and her eagerness to do anything but have dinner, Kaleb headed inside the house. He shut the front door just as Zaria walked out of her bedroom barefoot and dressed in nothing but a short white T-shirt and a pair of low-slung bikinis.

He didn't miss the sly smile on her face as she walked past him to take the hall leading into the kitchen. He bit his bottom lip as he shook his head. She knew damn well what she was doing and was enjoying the teasing.

"You want something to drink?" she called from the kitchen.

In that moment, he wanted to bend her over the sink and pull her panties down just enough to slide his hardness deep inside of her. "Uh, no . . . nothing for me," he said, deciding not to play with the heat in the kitchen and heading for the living room to take a seat.

There was a photo album open on the coffee

table, and Kaleb looked down at the pictures upon pictures of two identical girls from infancy to young adulthood. In many of them there were pictures of Zaria. Even though the twins aged, Zaria barely looked any different. *Is that her?* he wondered, leaning to peer closer at the photo.

The hairs on the back of his neck stood on end as Zaria entered the living room and came to sit beside him, holding a goblet of wine in her hand.

"The steaks are thawing and some corn on the cob is boiling," she said, tucking her feet beneath her carefully.

"Comfortable?" he asked, sitting back against the couch.

"Yes, thank you," she said, tilting her head to the side to watch him as she sipped her wine. "You?"

He nodded. "I'm good," he said, rubbing his chin before he unbuttoned his blazer.

"You're scared," she countered, dragging her fingertip around the rim of the goblet.

Kaleb frowned, his high brows deepening. "Of?"

Zaria leaned over to set her goblet on the coffee table and then untucked her feet to crawl on her hands and knees the short distance across the couch to him. She straddled his lap and rose up on her knees. "All of this," she said, motioning up and down her body.

Kaleb placed his hands on her soft thighs and then eased them up to settle on her hips. He leaned his head back against the couch, taking in the way her breasts were firm and high with her nipples hard and pressing against the thin material. Her plump mound was pressed against her bikini and tempting him, making him forget his plans for the evening. His plans for them. "Why would I be afraid when I know exactly what to do to all of this?" he asked, shifting his hand across to ease inside her bikini and stroke the warm and moist folds.

She gasped and thrust her hips forward as she moaned.

"Humph," he grunted in both pleasure and satisfaction as his eyes locked on to her face. He stroked her clit with his thumb and eased his index finger inside of her core.

Zaria raised her hands above her head and began to slowly circle her hips as she made love to his finger.

Kaleb awkwardly used his left hand to unbuckle his belt and then free his heated erection from his pants and boxers. He massaged the length of it as he eased his finger out just long enough to ease in two fingers.

He loved how uninhibited Zaria was as she continued to work her hips back and forth, causing her rigid walls to slide up and down his thick fingers.

She sighed as she reached for the edges of her T-shirt and pulled it over her head, her soft breasts lightly dropping back down against her chest. Her areolas were so deeply brown and round that his mouth watered to taste both.

He didn't fight the need.

Kaleb dipped his head and suckled her breasts into his mouth until it was full.

Zaria shivered and thrust her hips harder as she brought up a hand to massage and tease her own nipple.

Kaleb was just thinking about the condoms in his wallet when the front door opened and the sound of female voices mingled with their moans of pleasures. His eyes opened wide as he felt Zaria stiffen against him.

"Mama!" voices screeched.

Zaria covered her breasts with her arms as she fell off of Kaleb's lap, hit the couch, and then rolled onto the floor like a stuntwoman.

Mama!

"Seriously, Mama!"

"At least this one's her age," another feminine voice said.

"Or older with all that gray hair."

Kaleb's ego and erection deflated like air had been let out of a balloon. He watched as Zaria snatched up her T-shirt and pulled it over her head and jumped to her feet.

Unfortunately, the shirt was on backward.

"Go to your rooms and I'll be in there in a sec," Zaria said, trying to sound firm and look anything but crazy in her low-cut bikinis and awkwardly worn T-shirt that looked *completely* crazy.

Kaleb finished zipping away his flaccid manhood before standing up to face their unexpected audience. He didn't shy away from much easily, but seeing the full-grown twins from the photos standing there looking less than pleased shocked him. They looked to be in their early twenties. Zaria was *their* mother?

The one with her ebony hair in a ponytail threw her hands up into the air like she was in church and really feeling the spirit. "Lawd, he's young too?" she wailed comically.

The one with her hair cut into a bob crossed her slender arms over her chest. "Mama, you need to get it together," she said.

"Okay, enough," Zaria snapped, her voice hard and loud.

"These are your daughters?" Kaleb said, turning to look at her as if she were an alien as he pointed at the angry twins.

"Yes, Kaleb, these are my daughters, Meena and Neema."

He looked back at them, and they both gave him a nod and a glare.

"Excuse me," Zaria said, easing past him to hurry into her bedroom.

"You do know she's forty-two, right?" Meena asked, her tone very "so there."

No, he didn't know that. He visualized her body, that face, her style . . . the dress she'd worn earlier. Those were not the things a forty-something woman wore . . . or did . . . or showcased.

The twins still eyed him, and he was proud that he kept on his poker face.

"Okay, enough staring and glaring, ladies," Zaria said sternly as she walked back into the living room dressed in a velour sweat suit. She placed her hands on the small of their backs and gently pushed them out of the living room.

Kaleb watched Zaria the entire time. Even in her sweat suit, there was no denying the curves of her body and the sexiness of her appeal. He understood that forty was the new thirty but . . . "Damn, Zaria, you're forty-two?" he asked.

She nodded and shrugged. "Yes," she said simply. "Problem?"

He said nothing because he honestly didn't know if it was a problem. The only thing he knew for sure was it shocked the shit out of him. "I honestly thought you were my age," he admitted, hoping the distraction worked.

Zaria placed her hands on her hips and pretended to model for him. "I know for a fact that I look better than a lot of young chickies your age—including my ex-husband's wife," she said.

Kaleb looked behind him before he leaned against the back of the couch, his hands pushed into his pockets. "Are you over your ex?" he asked, thinking of the man dropping by her house without calling and then Zaria taking pleasure in insulting him. He was surprised at how the thought of that made him feel some kind of way.

Zaria froze and frowned at him. "I was over him the day he left me," she said, her eyes flashing with anger.

Kaleb saw that emotion clearly, and although a hundred more questions filled his head, he decided to just nod in understanding. "His loss," he said, meaning it.

"I can find good in the breakup because I found all of these things about myself that I wouldn't have if I'd stayed married to him," she said honestly. "I was all about being a wife and a mother and never put time into being a woman. In just being Zaria."

Kaleb squinted. "That's important," he said, decidedly guarded. His thoughts were racing even if his face didn't show it. Zaria's words were sinking in and giving him pause. A wife and a mother was exactly what he was looking for.

"Just doing me for once," Zaria said, doing a booty pop dance with a smile on her face.

Kaleb couldn't help but genuinely smile back at her. He gave in to the urge to wrap one arm around her waist and pull her body close to his.

Her hands landed on his shoulders and she leaned in toward him with a soft smile. "I'm sorry my daughters ruined our evening," she murmured against his mouth before kissing both corners of his mouth.

"I think we should take a rain check on dinner," Kaleb said, allowing his hands to lightly cup her buttocks.

"And dessert," she reminded him.

Kaleb made a face. "Dessert?"

Zaria nodded. "Cherries Jubilee," she whispered in his ear before biting his earlobe.

He enjoyed the shiver that raced over his body. "Never had it," he admitted.

Zaria leaned back and nodded as she bit her bottom lip. "Oh, you've had my cherry," she teased. "And it made you *very* jubilant."

Kaleb chucked as he nuzzled his face against her neck and got lost in her smell. Suddenly, he was both reluctant to leave her and anxious as hell to get away and think.

Chapter 7

Zaria closed the front door as Kaleb reversed his vehicle out of her yard and onto the main road. She had barely taken a deep breath when the twins' bedroom doors opened and they marched in like soldiers going to war. Zaria placed one hand on her hip and held the other up to them. "I'm not in the mood, ladies," she said, turning to head down the hall to the kitchen.

"How old is this one, Mama?" Meena asked.

Zaria knew it was Meena and not Neema because Meena's voice was slightly raspy, like a Jazz singer. "He's legal," she said, sliding the frozen steaks back into her deep freezer in the pantry across the room.

"That's not funny at all," Neema said.

Zaria recognized the slight lisp of her youngest twin daughter as she left the pantry and closed the door securely. "Listen, girls, I'm the mother and you're my children and guess what, I've raised you both. I don't call and aggravate you or snoop in your business or interfere like most mothers. I let you live your lives, so let me live mine." She paused when she saw them share a long look. "What?" she asked, moving over to the stove.

"Nothing," they said in unison.

"Should you really have men *here*?" Neema asked.

Zaria arched a brow. "*Here* is where I live," she countered.

"So did Daddy," Meena said, taking a small step back in her sneakers like she thought her mother just might come at her.

Zaria hated that she felt offended by their concern for their father. "*Did* is the operative word—and by his own choosing, thank you very much."

"You're both having a midlife crisis," Neema muttered, bouncing over to the fridge to pull out a personal jar of fruit punch.

Zaria cut her deep-set eyes from one to the other. "Stop worrying and fussing about me and your dad. I promise you that we're both just fine, girls. Okay?"

They both shrugged their slender shoulders.

"I was going to make steaks later when they defrosted, but what if I grill some turkey burgers to go with the corn on the cob?" she asked.

"No, that's okay. We came home to go to a party at the Armory," Meena said. "And, no, you cannot go—before you even ask."

Zaria shrugged one shoulder. "I had no plans to party this weekend . . . as you both clearly saw."

They groaned.

"I thought I had seen the last of those when we were breast-fed," Neema said in droll tones.

Zaria laughed as she took the pot of corn off the stove and poured out the steaming water from the pot. "Thank God they snapped back to life once I got the two of y'alls greedy behinds from tugging on them."

Neema threw her empty juice bottle into the recycling bin. "You and that silver-haired man serious?" she asked, placing the half-cooked corn on the cobs into a freezer-safe plastic container.

Zaria thought of Kaleb and smiled dreamily, even as she shook her head. "We're just friends. Nothing serious," she said honestly.

"Looked pretty serious to me," Meena said.

Zaria grabbed a dish towel to wipe down the stove. "Trust me, that was fun. All fun."

"So no stepdaddies who are just a few years older than us?"

Zaria eyed them both as if they were a pair of crazy aliens. "Trust and believe, the last thing on my mind is marriage."

She watched as they left the kitchen and headed back to their bedrooms.

They'd ruined her evening and they hadn't even come home for her. They were hunting up a party with their friends at the Walterboro National Guard Armory. And her first weekend off in a minute.

She strolled into the living room and plopped down onto the couch, grabbing the remote to turn on the television. But soon she bored of flipping through the channels—especially when she thought of having nothing else to do all night *but* channel surf.

When I could have been surfing Kaleb's—

"Mama, we're going."

She looked away from some reality television

show about brides competing for a wedding. They were in the same clothes with overnight bags on their shoulders. "You're not staying here tonight?" she asked.

Meena shook her head. "We're going back to our apartment. We both have to work tomorrow."

Zaria frowned. "I hate y'all riding that road all times of the night," she said, rising to her bare feet.

"We'll be fine, Ma," Neema said, coming over to kiss her cheek.

Meena followed suit. "And, no, we won't be drinking. We get high off of looking as good as our mama."

Zaria smiled at them as she walked them to the front door. "All right now," she said. "You know that's right."

As soon as they pulled off and flashed the lights at her, Zaria closed the front door and rushed over to snatch her phone from her purse.

She wondered just how far Kaleb had gotten as she dialed his cell phone number.

Kaleb picked up his cell phone from the passenger seat where he'd tossed it. At seeing Zaria's number, he set it back down and pressed his foot to the accelerator. Moments later, his phone vibrated and he knew she had left a voice mail.

Still, he pressed on toward Holtsville. Not even his curiosity made him return her call or check the message. His brain was filled with other thoughts, and he didn't want to process new information. Not yet.

Zaria's age.

Zaria's ex-husband.

Zaria's grown children.

Zaria's blasé attitude toward life.

"Shit," he swore, his eyes pensive as he slowed down to let a deer shoot out across the road. Late at night, deer were infamous for unexpectedly shooting from the woods and into the road, either crashing into oncoming traffic or causing unsuspecting drivers to swerve and wreck.

He checked to make sure it was alone before he accelerated forward. Kaleb was glad his thoughts weren't so filled that he had crashed.

Just as he entered the Holtsville town limits, his cell phone sounded off again. He ignored it as he came up on Donnie's Diner. His stomach grumbled as he remembered his feast of both food and Zaria had been interrupted by her daughters. Her *adult* daughters!

Shaking his head, he turned in to the small dirt-packed parking lot and shut off the engine. He was climbing out of the SUV when he spotted Jade's yellow Jeep Wrangler already parked. As soon as he walked into the diner his eyes searched the crowded tables for his brother Kaeden and Jade. He saw Jade but she was sitting with her mother, Deena.

When they spotted him, he headed in their direction, acknowledging those he knew from the small town with a nod before claiming a seat at their booth.

"Well, hello, stranger," Jade said with a big and bright smile. "You ever meet my mom, Deena?"

Kaleb's eyes took in the woman who looked

more like Jade's older sister than her mother.
"No, but I've seen pictures," he said, thinking everything about the woman reminded him of Zaria—even the look of interest in her eyes.

"Where have they been hiding you?" she said, extending her hand to him, her gold-painted nails flashing beneath the overhead lighting.

Jade sighed heavily.

"What?" Deena said innocently, taking great pleasure in sipping from the straw in her glass of lemonade.

Thinking one sexy cougar in his life was more than enough, Kaleb gave her a polite smile and turned his attention to his future sister-in-law. "Where's Kaeden?" he asked, looking up as the waitress came up to hand him a menu.

"He's at the house," she said. "He just called me."

Kaleb nodded. "I'll just have whatever dinner special y'all have," he told the waitress.

"Whatever you want, Kaleb," she said softly, looking at him directly with soft eyes that were filled with invitation.

He gave her a friendly smile and ignored the invite. He felt ashamed that he just remembered they'd shared a steamy one-night stand in the parking lot of the state fair in Ladson last October. "Good to see you," he added, feeling like a heel.

"It'll be good to see you again," she said, tucking the menu under her arm and sashaying away with lots of back-and-forth motion of her ample hips.

Kaleb turned to find two pairs of almost identical eyes looking at him in amusement. He just smiled bashfully and shrugged, knowing the women had peeped his connection to the waitress. "Anyway," he stressed.

"You Strong brothers are some bad boys," Jade said. "I'm glad I have mine locked down, 'cause the women flock like flies to shit."

"I want to get locked down," Kaleb insisted.

Jade's eyes widened.

Kaleb held up his hands. "Not with you," he said defensively. "My brothers and I don't share women."

Jade relaxed visibly. "Sorry."

Deena reached across the table to stroke his hands. "I have some keys that can lock—"

"Mother!" Jade snapped.

Kaleb deftly moved from her touch without it seeming apparent. Being hit on by his brother's future mother-in-law was very awkward. No matter that she looked just as fine and over forty as Zaria.

Deena just chuckled like she enjoyed his discomfort.

"So when do we get to meet the young lady stealing you away damn near every weekend?" Jade asked.

Kaleb shrugged. "I don't know if it's that serious," he said, shifting in his seat at Zaria being referred to as a "young lady."

Jade eyed him. "I thought the talk of the Strong clan was your search for Mrs. Right," she said. "Why waste time with Ms. Right Now?"

Kaleb looked away from Jade's inquisitive eyes. He watched Donnie, the owner and head cook of the diner, lumber his large frame over to the antique jukebox in the corner. Soon the sound of Roberta Flack and Donnie Hathaway filled the air.

Kaleb was an old soul when it came to music, and he recognized "I Who Have Nothing" instantly. Several of the diners rocked in their seats to the slow bluesy ballad that was love and soul and heartbreak all at once.

"Slow down, Donnie," someone called over to him.

Donnie just pumped his fist in the air and made his way back to the kitchen.

Kaleb looked out the window at the traffic slowly moving through Holtsville. He thought of Zaria. He remembered her undressing and then removing his shirt to press her body to his as her hands came up his back, her nails slightly etching his skin as she pressed one palm to the back of his head to pull his head down into the sweet groove of her neck as she pressed kisses to his shoulder.

They had stayed like that for the longest time, swaying back and forth, just lost in each other. Just swept up in their fire. Just enjoying the intimacy. No music. No words. Neither were needed.

The tender moment had come to him many times over the week. There was something in her caress that was beyond sexual. He could have stood there in her embrace, with her lips pressed to his flesh, all night.

He was glad when the image faded along with the song.

"If you miss her that much, why aren't you with her?" Deena asked softly.

Kaleb shifted his eyes to her. "I don't think we want the same things in life. She's older," he admitted.

"And?" Deena asked.

Kaleb leaned back in his chair as the waitress brought his steaming plate of food. His appetite was gone, but he pushed the food around with his fork. Stalling.

"And?" Deena asked again.

"She's forty-two with grown daughters," he said, setting down his fork and pressing his elbows onto the table.

"And?"

This time it was Jade who softly asked the one-word question.

Kaleb shrugged, wishing he hadn't said anything. He had barely wrestled with it alone and was far from ready for advice.

Zaria rose to her feet from her spot on Kaleb's porch as lights flashed from a vehicle turning into the yard. She felt nervous and anxious as she raked her fingers through her long hair and licked the last of the gloss from her lips.

She held up her hand to shield the light shining on her like a spotlight on a stage as Kaleb parked his SUV. She smiled, even as the lights remained on and he didn't move to exit the vehicle.

She playfully curtsied and bowed, wanting very badly to know what he was thinking as he sat there with his lights on her.

What seemed like minutes later, the lights

turned off and the SUV door opened. She moved down one step and then extended her foot to him. "I have on boots. I thought you could take me for that horseback ride in the morning," she said loudly as he stepped out of the shadow of the vehicle.

"What do you want out of this?" he asked, standing at the foot of the steps with his hands pushed deep into the pockets of his jeans.

Zaria lifted a brow. "What do you mean?"

Kaleb came up the steps until he stood on the one just beneath her. His eyes searched her face. "I told you I'm looking to settle down. Have a family. The whole happily-ever-after," he said.

Zaria couldn't help but fidget.

"Now, I know that you've been there and done that," Kaleb said.

She nodded. "Yes, that's very true."

Kaleb wiped his mouth. "This is just fun for you, right?"

Zaria moved to turn away from him, but he quickly reached out to grasp her arm. "I thought this was just fun for both of us," she told him, easing from his firm grip.

Kaleb nodded before taking a seat on the top step. "It is, but I wanted to see if maybe there was more that could grow between us," he admitted, pressing his elbows to his knees.

Zaria sat down beside him, linking her arm through one of his as she leaned her head against his shoulder. "We've only known each other a little over a month," she said gently. "Isn't it too soon to be anything more than what it is?"

Kaleb shrugged. "But I'm looking for someone to settle down with, and if that's not even a possibility for us, then why even bother?" he asked her, his eyes following the scurrying of some night creature across the front yard.

Zaria released a heavy breath. "I got married really young to a man a little older than me. He became my life. I was so happy being a housewife and eventually a mother. I thought my life was set, that everything was the way it was supposed to be. Eventually my girls graduated high school, and my husband who I loved a lot told me he was leaving me."

Zaria released a heavy breath. "I was devastated for the loss of my marriage and my life as I knew it. Suddenly I was without kids to raise and a husband to pamper and I felt so lost. So afraid. So alone. I realized I was so busy being a wife and a mother that I completely skipped just being Zaria."

Kaleb covered her hands with one of his own, his fingers stroking her skin softly.

"And so I started to live and enjoy all of the things I'd denied myself. I got a makeover, lost a few pounds, and got some new clothes. And I made a point of getting out there and enjoying life to the fullest. I wanted to have fun. To see what if feels like to do whatever I want, whenever I want."

Zaria lifted her head to look Kaleb in the eye. "I'm not ready to give that up," she told him with honesty.

Kaleb's eyes searched hers. "So my choice is to take it or leave it," he said.

Zaria smiled at him softly. "I don't want to lie to you or lead you on."

"But I'm not ready to say good-bye to you forever," he admitted.

Zaria gasped a little at the intensity of his words. She forced herself not to get swept away by them or him. "Then don't," she said. "This thing between us may run its course in a month or two. You can put your hunt for a wife on hold until then, right?"

Kaleb turned to look out at his farm in the distance. "If I meet a woman I think I can really have something with in that time, then I'll have to end things with you," he said, his voice firm as if he was trying to reassure her and himself.

Zaria thought of Kaleb with another woman, and a sharp wave of jealousy filled her. She'd given him her terms and he'd done the same. "I'm not ready to say good-bye to you forever either," she admitted softly.

Although they both struck a deal that put a time stamp on their relationship, Zaria and Kaleb made love with a slow and sensual intensity that brought tears to Zaria's eyes as she shivered with each climax he gave her. Long into the night, after they lay naked and entwined atop his sheets, they said nothing at all. They laid there with their eyes open and gazing out the window at the star-filled sky, thinking of everything that was and even more about everything that could never be. Both wondering if their time together would ever be enough.

* * *

Kaleb laughed at the sight of Zaria's body swamped in a pair of his old jeans and V-neck tee gathered at the waist with a huge belt. The addition of her high-heeled boots made the outfit all the more comical. Kaleb laughed until the muscles of his defined abdomen hurt.

"Not funny, Kaleb," Zaria said, coming across the bedroom to playfully swat his arm.

"You should have brought clothes," he said, holding his hands up.

Zaria turned and left his bedroom, holding the legs of the jeans off the floor with her hands.

"I wish I had a camera," Kaleb said, watching her and thinking that even swamped in oversized clothing with her hair up in a ponytail and her face free of makeup, the woman was still sexy.

That morning, it had been damn nice to wake up with her in his home. His bed. His arms.

"Okay, you really need a housekeeper," she called from the living room.

Kaleb smiled as he walked out of the bedroom behind her. "I know, but just about every weekend I'm getting a call to come to Summerville and lay up in someone else's home."

Zaria was bending over to fold the legs of the jeans, and Kaleb moved to stand behind her closely, grabbing her hips as he playfully imitated stroking her doggy style. She giggled as she joined him in his play and threw her hips back.

"Get it, Daddy. Get it, Daddy. Unh!" Zaria chanted.

"If we don't stop, I'm going in those big-ass

pants you have on," Kaleb told her, pressing his long erection against her buttocks.

Zaria looked back at him over her shoulder, wide-eyed, before she raced away from him and into the kitchen. She didn't stop until she was on the other side of the island.

Kaleb looked over at her face, pretty and vibrant, with her eyes sparkling in humor. She looked radiant and beautiful. "You know we can ride horses anytime," he said, undoing his belt and unzipping his pants.

Zaria shook her head and ignored the sight of the length of him against his thigh in his snug-fitting boxers. "I am sore," she told him, raising her hands as he kicked his pants away with a comically lecherous wiggle of his brows as he advanced on her.

"Nothing like a good massage to work away any soreness," he told her, coming around the island.

"Who says I want any this morning?" she said.

"Yeah, right," he countered, turning the corner. He stopped dead in his tracks to find that behind the cover of the island, Zaria had already dropped the jeans and her panties down around her ankles.

She bent over the island as she wiggled her bare bottom.

Kaleb rushed out of his boxers and came to stand behind her, settling the length of his hardness between her buttocks. "Perfect fit, huh?" he asked, bending down to kiss her neck as he rocked his hips back and forth, sending his dick up and down that smooth and warm valley.

Zaria nodded in agreement as she circled her hips.

"Rise and shine, Bubba!"

Zaria gasped deeply and Kaleb froze at the sudden sound of footsteps and voices. "Not again," she wailed, using a strong push with her buttocks to back Kaleb away before she ducked down to hide behind the island.

His three brothers turned and faced him. Kaleb wasn't happy at all to see them, even though all were as thick as thieves. "I really need to lock my door."

Kaleb grabbed the jeans Zaria had on and rushed into them. "Hey, I'ma need y'all to hit me up later—"

"What's this about you doing some old lady?" Kahron asked.

Zaria plucked Kaleb's shin.

Kaleb dropped his head to his chest.

"Jade told me the little lady you been hiding away is the same age as her mom," Kaeden added, opening the fridge to look inside.

"Yeah, the little old lady," Kade teased, jumping up to sit his tall frame on the top of the island.

"Does she breast-feed you—"

"That's enough!" Kaleb said sharply. "Grow the hell up."

The brothers all frowned and eyed each other. "Lighten up. We're just joking," Kade said, ever the peacemaker.

Zaria stood up beside Kaleb, being sure to lower the T-shirt down around her hips. "They're just jokes," she said sweetly.

The look of surprise on his brothers' faces was classic. Kaleb crossed his arms over his chest and braced his hip against the edge of the island as Zaria tossed her hair and gave each of them a sultry wink before she turned and kissed him with an exaggerated moan.

He could barely keep a smile off his face as she went around the island to walk up to each one with her hand extended. "I'm Zaria, the little old lady, and you are?" she asked Kahron.

"Kahron . . . ma'am," he said, shaking her hand.

She moved in front of Kade, sitting on the island. "And you?"

Kade slid off the island and removed his baseball cap, exposing his silver curls. "I'm Kade."

She turned to Kaeden and patiently waited.

He cleared his throat and pressed his hand into hers. "I'm Kaeden."

Kaleb loved that she didn't seem at all embarrassed about being in nothing but an oversized T-shirt that barely covered her shapely bottom and the top of her thighs.

"Oh, there's a *K* thing going on. Cute," she said, before shifting her amused eyes to Kaleb. "I'll be in the bedroom."

She bent over and hunched her back and pretended to use a cane as she walked away like the old woman they accused her of being. The sound of her delighted laughter sounded just before Kaleb's bedroom door shut.

Kaleb chuckled at the look of surprise still on their faces. "Besides being made fools out of, what can I help you with?" He scooped up his discarded jeans and boxers, then grabbed Zaria's delicate lace panties from the floor as well, sliding them into his pocket.

"No wonder you're sniffing around her tail so hard," Kade said, sliding his cap back on his head.

"We're just friends," Kaleb told them.

Kade looked at him. "But what about your plans?" he asked.

"I'm still looking for the one."

The three brothers headed for the front door.

"We'll see you at church?" Kaeden asked.

Kaleb shook his head. "I doubt it but I'm coming for dinner," he said.

"Sorry about that," Kade said, tapping his fist against Kaleb's before he walked out the door.

As soon as they were gone, Zaria came back out of the room, still dressed in the T-shirt. "You and your brothers sure are a handsome bunch," she said. "So you're all prematurely gray?"

Kaleb nodded. "My sister Kaitlyn, too, but she dyes it. We get it from our dad."

"It works for y'all," she said, coming over to wrap her arms around his waist.

Kaleb pressed a kiss to her temple as he wrapped one strong arm around her. "My mom and sisters-in-law cook a big dinner every Sunday . . . Do you want to go with me?"

She didn't answer for a long time, and he felt the tension in her body. "I don't think that's a good idea," she finally said.

Kaleb felt intensely disappointed but he didn't show it as he scooped her up into his arms. "No biggie," he lied. "Let's get you dressed and let me show you the farm."

Zaria buried her face into his neck as he carried her back into the bedroom.

Zaria leaned against the paddock fence, amazed as Kaleb rode the stallion as if their bodies were united. She was intrigued by the strength and control he used while still having a gentle quality and respect for the animal. A piece of her regretted turning down his offer to ride with him.

She grew up in the South, but her upbringing had been far from the rural nature of a little town like Holtsville, where there was more dirt than concrete and life definitely moved at a more laid-back pace. And she could tell that Kaleb loved his farm and was proud of his accomplishments.

And for his young age, he should be proud. She'd met men twice his age with less drive and ambition.

As the wind blew up loose dirt, she covered her face with her shirt, knowing she would need a trip to her hairstylist to get her weave thoroughly washed and restyled. But it was worth it to see Kaleb in his element.

As he steered the horse toward her at a slow trot, she smiled and waved at him. "You handle a horse well, Kaleb," she called up to him.

"Sure you don't want to go for a ride?" he asked, his voice seeming even more deep and powerful.

Zaria shook her head. "I'm good."

Kaleb laughed.

When his eyes shifted up to look off into the

distance beyond her, Zaria turned to follow his gaze. Her eyes opened a bit in surprise at the four-wheeler coming toward them. They opened wider to see an older woman in her midfifties steering the vehicle with a teenaged girl by her side.

Zaria knew it was Kaleb's mother. She looked down at her oversized clothing now dusty and wrinkled and unkempt. Her hair was windblown and fuzzy. She knew she looked a hot mess. She glanced at Kaleb and he gave her an apologetic shake of his head.

"Hi, Uncle Kaleb," the teenage girl shouted with an enthusiastic wave of her hand.

The four-wheeler slowed to a stop. The woman, with her skin barely weathered and her silky silver hair cut in a stylish short style, stepped down easily and came up to Zaria with a smile on her face and her hand extended. "So you're the gal keeping my son all tied up lately," she said, her voice strong and filled with no nonsense.

Wiping her hand on her jeans, Zaria shook the woman's hand. "I'm Zaria. Zaria Ali," she said.

"Call me Lisha, and this is my eldest grand-baby, Kadina," Lisha said as the teen stepped forward.

Zaria eyed her. "Let me guess—you're Kade's daughter," she said. "You look just like him."

Kadina smiled like a teen beauty pageant contestant. "Everybody says that," she said, even as she side-eyed Zaria's get-up.

"Kaleb said my clothes were too fancy to wear around the ranch," she explained.

Lisha cut her son a chastising eye. "He could

have gotten something from my daughter Kaitlyn for you."

"Yeah, Uncle Kaleb," Kadina added, walking over to easily climb atop the fence to pet the nose of the horse in her shorts and tank top.

"Kaleb, why don't you take Kadina for a ride?" Lisha suggested gently.

"Zaria and I are just friends. No need for the third degree, Ma," Kaleb said, shifting in his saddle.

"I'm not going to grill her, Kaleb. Don't be silly." Lisha waved her hand dismissively.

"Come on, Uncle Kaleb," Kadina said, standing on the top rung of the fence to climb onto the saddle behind her uncle. She placed her arms behind her to hold the notch on the cantle of the saddle.

Zaria saw Kaleb give his mother a strong and stern look before he guided the horse into a gallop.

"You know I love my family, Zaria," Lisha began, leaning against the hood of the four-wheeler.

Zaria remained silent and turned her gaze to watch Kaleb and his niece on the horse, even as her heart raced.

"Kaleb is my quiet son, my reflective son. He loves easily and deeply even when he doesn't show it," she continued. "And when he finds that special woman, he will love her deeper than any sea God ever created."

Zaria thought of the way he held her as they slept or the way he blessed her with kisses for no reason at all, and she could believe his mother's words. Kaleb had the build and the stance of a fighter, but deep down he was a lover.

"Now, y'all age difference don't mean nothing to me as long as you two are on the same page," Lisha said.

Her tone made Zaria look over at her.

Lisha smiled but her eyes were steely when she said, "Just make sure you're both on the same page. You hear?"

Translation: *Don't hurt my son.*

Zaria got the message clearly.

CHAPTER 8

Three months later

Zaria checked her hair in the rearview mirror at the red light before accelerating her white VW Bug forward when the light changed to green. She glanced at the digital clock on the dash and made a face.

She was supposed to have met Kaleb thirty minutes ago. She had called twenty minutes ago to say she was on the way. Another five minutes passed before she finally pulled into the parking lot of the Gaillard Theatre in Charleston. As soon as she raced across the parking lot in her four-inch heels and skintight dress, she saw Kaleb standing out front pacing and glancing at his watch.

"I made it," she said, breathless as she eyed how handsome he looked in all black.

"I swear you're going to be late to your own funeral, Zaria," he told her.

She frowned, thinking he sounded more like

her father than her friend. "Let's just go in," she said, pulling the glass door open and walking in ahead of him.

Kaleb caught up to her and slid his arm around her waist. "Hey," he said softly, pressing a kiss to her cheek. "Thanks for coming."

Zaria softened her stance. "Let's just go in and enjoy the show. Okay?" she asked, giving him a soft peck on the corner of his mouth.

In truth, Zaria was beginning to feel like her life was in a rut. She went to work, came home, and prepared to spend whatever free time she had with Kaleb. Nothing much else differed. She couldn't even remember the last time she went out dancing. Her world was becoming wrapped up in Kaleb, and that worried her. It was a road she didn't want to travel again, especially since she knew their interlude was just that. There was no forever and happily-ever-after for them.

She never thought they would be together even this long . . . and she was considering ending things because she felt herself getting attached. They began leaving the solitude of each other's homes and doing more things together. Dinners. Plays. Walks in the park. Trips to the beach.

Somewhere along the line, their casual and flirty affair began feeling and looking more like a full-blown relationship. As much as she enjoyed his company, she wasn't looking to be half of a couple. But that was exactly what they had become.

And knowing he wanted more from her than she was ready to give, his mother's words of warning haunted more and more of late: *As long as you're both on the same page . . .*

But were they?

As Kaleb lightly guided her to their seats, Zaria fought the urge to shake off his touch. Dating younger men had meant she had the control in the relationship, but that wasn't the case with Kaleb. He was a man's man, and of late she had easily slipped into the role of following his lead.

That was yet another no-no.

Her control in the relationship was gone. She was used to younger men who jumped when she said jump, who catered to her and answered her silly whims. She liked molding them into what she wanted.

Kaleb Strong was having none of that.

Zaria remembered when she first asked him to go out at two a.m. to get her favorite ice cream. Kaleb had politely but firmly let her know that there was no ice cream on earth good enough to make anyone in their right mind go searching for it at two in the morning.

That was a first. Zaria had made the demand before in the past, and other, far more willing young men had fulfilled her request with amusing eagerness.

As the lights dimmed and the chatter of the small crowd faded, the curtains opened, showing a large band and a lone microphone in the center of the stage. Jazz music soon filled the air, and the audience applauded as a quartet strolled onto the stage singing in harmony.

Zaria settled her elbow on the armrest between them and set her chin in her hand as Kaleb draped his arm across the back of her seat. As he began to tap his foot in time to the music, Zaria felt herself being lulled to sleep. Several times she caught her eyes closing and her elbow almost slipping off the armrest.

The combination of a hard week at work, sometimes working days with near double shifts, and the fact that she preferred the energy and flow of hip-hop over jazz took what could have been just slight boredom to Kaleb gently shaking her awake.

"Huh? What? I wasn't asleep," she protested as she sat up straight and wiped a thin line of drool from her chin. Several people around her turned to glare or shhh her.

She looked over at Kaleb and then down at the unmistakable wet spot on his shoulder. *Damn, I was sleeping that hard,* she thought.

"You were snoring louder than a grizzly bear," he whispered in her ear.

Zaria was flooded with embarrassment, imagining the scene she made. "I'm sorry," she mouthed to him, somewhat relieved to see the hint of a smile around his mouth.

Still, for the remaining hour of the concert, Zaria did everything she could to focus and try to enjoy what she knew was good music. She chewed gum. She crossed and uncrossed her legs. She shifted in her seat. She sighed. She scratched her scalp. She took off her shoes and slipped them back on.

Basically, she knew for a fact that as much as Kaleb enjoyed himself, the whole jazz thing wasn't her cup of tea.

When the performers took their final bows and the audience gave them a standing ovation, Zaria hurried to her feet.

"Was that as torturous for you as it seemed?" Kaleb asked as they filed out of the auditorium with the rest of the crowd.

Zaria looked up at him and bit back a smile. "I'm sorry. You would think the fortysomething would be the one to love jazz, but it's not my thing. I'm sorry," she said again, reaching out to lightly grab his arm.

"It's cool," he said.

He loves easily and deeply even when he doesn't show it.

Zaria wondered what other emotions Kaleb kept to himself. Was he truly angry or disappointed and just not showing it?

They reached the outside, and the summer breeze felt and smelled delicious as they strolled along with the crowd toward their parking spot. She enjoyed just being at his side, just being surrounded by his presence and getting lost in his scent. And it filled her with so many mixed emotions.

Kaleb Strong was a dangerous man. Not violent or mean or destructive by any measure, but he was completely loveable. Totally addictive. Achingly satisfying.

And that was all wrong for something casual and temporary.

"You hungry?" Kaleb asked, the light from the lampposts causing the silver flecks of his hair to shimmer.

"No, but these heels were not made for this

long journey back to the car," she joked, fighting the urge to kick off the stilettos and walk barefoot.

Kaleb pointed. "My SUV is right there. I'll drive you to your car."

Zaria nearly fainted in relief because her pinky toe was catching all kinds of hell!

As soon as he opened the door and helped her up into the seat, Zaria kicked off her shoes. When Kaleb gently twisted her around and took one of her feet into his hands to massage it, Zaria leaned forward and planted a kiss on the top of his head, inhaling the scent of his shampoo.

He tilted his head up and smiled a little before kissing her in the most casually intimate way before looking back down at the work he put in on her feet.

Just as long as you're both on the same page . . .

A man like Kaleb Strong deserved to be loved, to be a father and a husband. To have a wife who looked at him with the same love and devotion that he gave her.

Zaria felt breathless, and tears filled her eyes as she was overcome with an overwhelming sadness—not only did she know that she would never be that woman, but also she was possibly stopping him from finding the one to complete him.

"Let's go dancing," she told him, swallowing down the emotion filling her throat.

Kaleb frowned as he looked at her. "At a club?" he said.

"Yes, at a club," Zaria said with enthusiasm. "Let's go have fun—I mean, more fun."

Kaleb laughed as he stepped forward to grab

her thighs with both his hands. "And then what?" he whispered against her mouth.

Zaria shivered like she was naked in the cold, when just like that his nearness made her hot, as if she were standing in fire. She brought her hand up and cupped the side of his strong and handsome face, tilting her chin up to trace his mouth with her tongue. "And then we go back to my place. Deal?"

She was pleasantly surprised when he nodded in agreement with one last taste of her mouth. Kaleb Strong was not a man easily convinced to do something he didn't want to do. He was nothing like her Hot Boyz jumping and bending to her whims with the flexibility of a strand of grass in wind.

He was nothing like most men his age at all.

"You sure we're not overdressed?" Kaleb asked as they walked up to the entrance of Club Imagine in North Charleston.

"No," Zaria told him, grabbing his wrist to lead him inside the club.

Kaleb watched her. She was already grooving side to side as they stood in line, as if she couldn't wait to hit the dance floor. All of the sleepiness she had earlier was gone.

Although he was the younger of the two, she was far more excited than him to get in a club. It had never really been his thing. He was a country boy who loved farming, hunting, and working with his hands. Sipping on drinks, and posted up on the wall while profanity-laced music blared hard enough to give a dead man life never turned him on.

He paid their entrance fee and let Zaria guide him into the dimly lit club. It reminded him of the first night he met her while she was bartending and he had sat up in the club waiting to see if she had caught on and cared about his hint that he would be waiting for her there.

Zaria didn't even bother with a table as she tucked her purse under her arm and started dancing to some bass-driven rap song, saying, "That's my song right there!"

Kaleb tried to keep up with her with his little two-step, but Zaria had his mouth opening more and more in shock as she did all the current dances. When she did the Dougie with the energy of a fifteen-year-old, he knew he couldn't keep up with her. She liked to party, and he could look around the dance floor and see that a lot of men—young, old, and pretending not be old—were watching her.

She made a sight with her waist-length weave, flashy makeup, and dangling earrings. Her gold satin skirt showed off her legs as she did the wind and grind like she was on a job.

The skirt was so short—and the men were looking so closely—that he wondered if they were catching an occasional glimpse of her hidden pleasures.

Zaria danced up to him and then turned to press her buttocks to him as she pressed his hands to her hips as she worked them back and forth enough to make a belly dancer check her skills. She wrapped her arms around his neck, but Kaleb was too busy worrying that raising her arms was also raising her clothes higher.

He knew he had no right to feel jealous. Zaria wasn't his girlfriend, and she even encouraged him to still be on the lookout for a nice girl to get serious with, but the thought of Zaria dancing that way in clubs, with other men, dressed scantily, and maybe even taking one of them home like she did him made his entire chest burn like he had a furnace in his chest. A furnace fueled with jealousy and possessiveness.

Two things he had no right feeling when they both agreed to enjoy it for what it was while it was still fun.

"Ohhhh, that's my jam," Zaria said, cupping her hand to her mouth as she rapped along with Biggie's classic "Juicy," word for word.

That made him smile as he watched her making the hand motions and all like she was onstage. Forty-two really wasn't that old, he thought, still doing his two-step and trying to keep up with her.

Two hours later, Kaleb begged off another dance and claimed a seat. He glanced at his watch and did a double take to see it was close to three in the morning. He ordered a shot of vodka on the rocks from the waitress walking around the crowded club, carrying it with him outside for some fresh air.

As soon as he stepped onto the sidewalk, he felt a million times better. The air wasn't filled with different colognes and perfumes mingling in the air with body funk, alcohol, and body odors. But the steady *thump-thump* of the music's bass still sounded loudly.

He sipped from the clear plastic cup, wincing just a bit as it went down.

"Just please come get me."

Still holding his cup to his mouth, he turned to see a pretty girl with a short hairdo of mostly flips pacing as she talked into her phone. He was curious as he watched her.

"We went to the concert, and when it was over, she said she was stopping by here for a quick drink. That was damn near three hours ago," she said, her voice filled with annoyance. "I'm ready to go and she talking about shutting the club down."

Sounds like my night, he thought.

"Just come and get me," she pleaded with someone, eventually sighing and flipping her cell phone closed before she tossed it back into her clutch with the speed a pitcher would lob a fastball.

"I hate clubs," she said, looking up and seeing Kaleb's curious eyes on her. She sounded slightly apologetic.

He nodded in understanding before tossing the rest of his drink onto the brick-paved street. He balled the cup up with a strong hand.

"I guess your girlfriend is still in there dancing, too, huh?" she asked, stepping up to stand beside him.

"She's not my girlfriend," he said, but quickly added, "but we're here together."

She nodded. "I saw y'all at the jazz concert and then inside," she told him.

Kaleb eyed her. "Did you like it? The music? Did you enjoy it?" he asked.

"Yessss," she said, her smile spreading. "I

bought the ticket and since I'm single, I brought my cousin. She drove and now we're *here.*"

She said "here" like it was akin to the plague.

"Did you like it?" she asked.

Kaleb tossed the balled up cup into the air and caught it several times. "I love jazz."

"Yeah, me too. In fact, I play the piano."

Kaleb looked impressed. "Wow, that's cool."

"Yeah."

They fell silent.

Kaleb thought of Zaria. "I better go in and check on her," he said, turning to head back into the club. The feel of a hand touching his arm caused him to look back.

She pressed a business card into his hand. "I hope I'm not being disrespectful to your friend, but, um, if things don't develop . . . maybe you can call me?"

Kaleb looked down at the business card but he didn't take it. She pushed it into his hand before walking past him back into the club. He looked down at it.

HEATHER LONG
ATTORNEY-AT-LAW
843-555-1212

There was no future for him and Zaria. She made it plain that marriage and motherhood wasn't a part of her future. And he told her that if he met someone he thought could be the woman for him, he would end things with Zaria and pursue his future. Still, it didn't feel right taking numbers from another woman while he was on a date with Zaria.

Even though Heather could have been a good candidate for compatibility.

Even though he saw more and more over the weeks that outside of the bedroom, he had nothing in common with the sexy older woman.

Even though his desire to be a father seemed to be increasing every day.

Even though he knew that his days with Zaria were numbered.

Kaleb folded the card and then balled it up in his hand with the cup. He turned and found Zaria standing there watching him closely, her hair slightly plastered to her head and her face damp with sweat.

Zaria's eyes darted down to his hand and he knew that she had seen the other woman give him the card, but she said nothing about it.

"That club was packed," she said, walking toward him to press a hand to his chest and look up at his handsome and strong square face. "Thank you for bringing me even though I can tell it was the last place you wanted to be."

Kaleb nodded as he moved past her to throw the cup and the card into the large trash can on the side of the building. He looked at Zaria with clear intent.

She just shifted her gaze away. "If it's cool with you, I'm just going to head home alone. I'm pretty tired," she said.

Kaleb nodded even though he felt disappointed.

"I'm going to follow you to make sure you get in safe," he said, sounding casual and normal.

He was surprised when she didn't even kiss him before she climbed into her VW and started the engine. Pausing for just a second, he climbed into his SUV and soon he was pulling out of the parking lot behind her.

As he followed her the short distance to her house, he was deep in thought. He had to admit that although he had no regrets about tossing the card, it did make him wonder if he would ever find the one he could settle down with if he was giving respect to a woman he was casually involved with.

As their time together went on, the fiery passion between them remained just as strong as their first night together—if not stronger. But the differences between them were becoming more and more clear. And more than the fact that he wanted to settle down and Zaria was enjoying the second half of her life being free.

But mostly—and most importantly—even if they got beyond their age difference and the fact that her kids had shown him nothing but cold indifference any time he encountered them, what kind of life would they have if he grew to resent her for the children she wouldn't have? Would she spend some weekend partying in the club while he was home worrying that her gyrations drew the leers of men?

Kaleb sighed. Zaria had never turned down a chance for them to be intimate. Never. And that let him know that she felt some kind of way about seeing him talking to that woman outside the club. Still, he refused to make himself believe she was jealous because she cared deeply for him. The most Zaria Ali wanted from him was hanging between his thighs.

Maybe it was time to leave it alone and focus on his future. He couldn't dwell in these shades of gray with her much longer. He was more than a damn sex toy for an older woman out looking for nothing more than fun.

Zaria stood at her window and watched Kaleb reverse his SUV and then pull out of her yard. When his brake lights flashed like a pair of angry red eyes, she pulled the curtain back. Her heart stopped in her chest, and all of her conflicting emotions raced through her as she waited for his next move.

Come back.

No, go.

Come to me, Kaleb.

No, go home. Just go home.

She closed her eyes, leaning her head against the windowpane. When she opened them just a few seconds later, he was gone.

Kaleb sat propped up on pillows, flipping through the cable channels barely long enough to recognize a familiar face of a show he wanted to see. The digital box said it was four in the morning, and after a long day on the farm, the jazz concert, and a few hours in the club that felt like time wasted out of his life that he couldn't get back, he still wasn't tired.

His thoughts were filled with Zaria as he went back and forth like a swinging pendulum between leaving her alone to move on with his life and enjoying whatever time they had together.

Still . . . although he hadn't been looking for a woman like Heather, it did remind him that his goal was to find a woman who was the total package and more than just incredible sex.

The more he weighed his options, the less he knew what he wanted to do. He was just as confused and undecided as before.

That next morning, Zaria was surprised to find she couldn't sleep. She had tossed and turned all night, plagued with dreams of Kaleb and the cutie from outside the club running down their wedding aisle hand in hand with smiles on their faces. She was glad when the sun finally glared against her face and she was able to kick off the covers to start what she hoped would be a better day.

It went from bad to worse.

She usually had her mound freshly waxed, but in the days of being caught up in Kaleb and him telling her he liked the slight peach fuzz, Zaria hadn't been for her monthly trip to the spa. She was studying her body in the mirror when she caught the glimmer of something in the short curly hairs between her thighs. She brushed it, thinking it was a piece of string from her towel, but when the white fleck remained, Zaria made a face filled with horror. "Oh, hell no!" she snapped, grabbing her makeup mirror that magnified everything ten times.

She inhaled so deeply in shock that she knew she had sucked dust particles and everything else into her lungs. "A gray hair . . . down there! What the hell?"

Zaria dropped the mirror onto the sink and closed her eyes to force herself to breathe slowly and calmly. She eyed her tube of mascara but pushed the crazy idea of dying *that* hair.

There was no way she would let Kaleb eyeball that. She hurried from the bathroom and grabbed her cordless phone to make an appointment for a full body wax—she wasn't taking any chances. Next she dialed Hope. When she got no answer, she called the more rambunctious Chanci.

"Hey you," Chanci said.

"Girl, how 'bout I'm going silver down below," Zaria drawled sarcastically, reaching for her robe to pull on and tie securely.

Chanci laughed and laughed like she had Kevin Hart doing stand-up just for her.

Zaria arched a brow. "This is not funny, Chanci. Wait until you get one or two or a few."

"Girl, please, been there and done that. No biggie," she said.

Zaria could just see her friend waving her hand like she didn't have a care in the world. "Why didn't you tell me?"

"Because it's no biggie and you wouldn't be so

shell-shocked if you stopped dying the hell out of the few gray hairs you got on your head."

Zaria sucked air between her teeth and plopped down onto the commode. "Well, I have already made an appointment to have that baby removed."

"Girl, you are conceited."

"Yes, I know," Zaria said, imitating J. J. Evans from the 1970s sitcom *Good Times.*

Chanci just laughed. "So how's Lover Boy?"

Zaria thought of Kaleb and she smiled. "He . . . he deserves to fall in love with a woman his age who wants to get married and have his beautiful babies," she admitted.

"So you still don't want to get married to him . . . *one day* and have his beautiful babies . . . *one day*?"

Zaria shook her head. "I am forty-two years old. Are you kidding me?"

"What? I'll have you know that Jennifer Lopez and Halle Berry had their first children after forty. Vivica Fox did an interview saying she wants a baby with her younger man, and you are way younger than Auntie Viv, boo-boo. Girl, get with the time. Your eggs are far from dried."

Zaria shook her head. "Listen, I am too old to even think about putting myself into one of these baby daddy situations. I have raised my kids. No more babies for me."

"So are you going to end it and get out of the way of all these young girls willing to snatch him up in a heartbeat, or are you going to realize that you really care for this man? And when you admit that to yourself, it changes *everything*. Trust and believe that."

* * *

Kaleb enjoyed the feel of the wind beating against his face and upper body as he used his thighs and the reins to control his horse. He barely saw the great expanse of trees and flatlands he passed as he galloped at full speed. He left his brothers behind with ease.

Of all his brothers, Kaleb loved riding horses the most. At times he could be seen on one of his horses throughout Holtsville, preferring it to cars or ATVs. Growing up, he had been the one most likely to be found in the stables with the horses. He loved their quiet strength.

As he slowed the stallion down to a trot, he lightly patted his neck, feeling his racing pulse mirror his own. He came to a stream running through his acreage and dismounted to walk him toward it to drink. He heard the hoofbeats of his brothers' horses nearing and turned to watch them dismount and lead the horses to the water as well.

"You have something to prove?" Kade joked, taking his hat off to wipe some of the sweat from his fine silver curls.

Kaleb just laughed before taking a seat on a large flat stone. "Just some stuff on my mind," he admitted, looking up at Kade and Kahron as he squinted his eyes against the sun. His youngest brother, Kaeden, was happily ensconced in his office, busy with facts and figures as an accountant. He missed the farming gene completely.

"Is this about your woman drama?" Kahron

asked, shifting his ever-present aviator shades on his face.

"No, it's about those damn shades. Do you wear them when you sleep?" Kaleb snapped, reaching for a pebble to toss into the river with a *plop*.

Kade looked between them and shook his head. "Go 'head, Kaleb," he urged.

He shook his head and remained quiet, keeping his thoughts to himself. His brothers knew him well, and they left him to his thoughts, turning their conversation with each other to the upcoming livestock auction.

Reaching for another pebble, Kaleb skipped it across the water with the skill taught to him as a youth by his father. Kaleb thought of his parents, their family, their love and happiness. Even through arguments and petty squabbles, the Strongs always had each other's backs. It was one for all and all for one.

Kaleb had faced the fact that somewhere along the line of fun and frivolity, his feelings for Zaria had become quite serious. Everything had changed for him, and that meant he had even more to lose.

CHAPTER 9

There was a disconnect. They both felt it.

Zaria sat up and covered her breasts with her arms as she looked down at Kaleb with his hardness still deep within her walls. "This is the end of the road, huh?" she asked, her voice husky and soft.

Kaleb covered his eyes with his forearm. "I have never wanted any woman as much as I want you, Zaria," he admitted.

"*But* . . . it's the end of the road?" she repeated.

Kaleb remained silent.

Zaria laughed bitterly. "So what was this? One last good screw for the road?" she asked.

Kaleb removed his arm to look up at her in disbelief. "Get off, Zaria," he said, moving to roll from under her.

Zaria locked her knees to his side and began to roll her hips. "No, I wanna make sure you get this happy ending."

Kaleb reached out and grabbed her upper arms. "Get. Off," he ground out between clenched teeth before he literally lifted her off of his dying erection and then sat on the side of her bed to drop his silver-flecked head in his hands.

Zaria pulled her knees to her chest, watching him. "Is she the one?" she asked, sounding casual and friendly . . . and phony.

Kaleb looked at her over his broad shoulder. "Who?"

"The little cutie from outside the club that night. Is she the one?" Zaria asked, reaching for her wrinkled top sheet to pull up around her nudeness.

Kaleb rose from the bed, his buttocks flexing as he walked over to grab his clothes from the floor. "I wouldn't disrespect you like that, Zaria," he said.

She watched him jerk on his clothes roughly. "Why? I'm not your lady," she said.

Kaleb's eyes flittered over her face as he stood there with his shirt in his hands and his jeans slung low on his narrow hips. "That was your choice, not mine. Remember?"

"Maybe she can give you all them babies you want," she said. "And go to the jazz concerts and complain about clubs with you and just be nice and boring with you."

He locked his eyes on her. She'd heard their conversation.

"Don't insult me, Zaria," he demanded in a hard voice.

"So is this it, then? You sure you don't wanna have one last fuck for the road?" she asked, her voice low.

Kaleb frowned and squinted his eyes at her. "I

would hope sex wouldn't be the last thing you offered me after close to six months dealing with each other, Zaria," he told her coldly.

"Why?" she asked. "Let it end how it began, right?"

His face became incredulous. "Why are you doing this?" he asked. "You let that bullshit your husband pulled on you—which is more about his crap than yours—mess you up that bad?"

Zaria leaned back a bit, offended. "Leave my ex out of this."

"Why don't *you* leave your ex out of this—out of your life, out of your decisions," he bit back, pointing his finger at her. "You actually believe everything you do is some show of liberation and claiming yourself and all that crap when all you're trying to do is prove to him that you could have been what he wanted."

Zaria glared at Kaleb before she flung back the covers and hopped out of the bed to stalk over to him. "You don't know what the hell you're talking about, Kaleb Strong, so keep your nickel-and-dime analysis to your damn self," she snapped before she turned and strode across her bedroom.

He followed behind her and grabbed her arm to turn her around. "If it's not, then why are you trying to be younger and sexier?"

"Go to hell," she spat. "I don't even know why we started this."

"Me neither," Kaleb shot back in anger.

Zaria stood up straight and eyed him. "Hey, it's simple enough to end it. There's no need for all this drama."

"You're all about drama," he muttered, waving his hand at her in agitation as he jerked his black wife-beater tee over his head.

"What the hell does that mean?"

Kaleb let out a short sarcastic laugh as he eyed her and then grabbed his genitals. "This is all you ever wanted from me, even when I was willing to give you more, and now just the thought of me moving on to someone who wants more makes you start some stupid argument. For what? Drama, that's what."

Zaria outstretched her arms. "What do you want from me? To pretend I'm not forty-two?"

Kaleb looked incredulous. "You do that anyway, with your skintight clothes and high heels up in the club doing the gotdamned Dougie and partying with women young enough to be your daughter."

That felt like an emotional gut punch. "Better than getting old before your time, Mr. Farmer in the Flipping Dell."

"Go to hell, Zaria," he said coldly before moving past her to leave the bedroom.

"Don't you walk away from me, Kaleb Strong," she said, coming around to step in his path to the front door, still just as naked as the day she was born.

Kaleb stepped back from her. "When are you going to grow up?" he asked, his annoyance clear.

"And what is that supposed to mean?"

Kaleb sighed and wiped his face with his hand as he shook his head in disbelief. "Never mind, because I'm not even sure what this dumb-ass argument is really about—and neither are you."

Zaria hated how helpless she felt. She hated that she wanted him to stay. She hated the jealousy she felt. She hated that the thought of never seeing him made her feel like she was drowning.

She closed her eyes as tears welled up. She pointed her finger at him as she struggled with the words. "I'm sorry, Kaleb. I am sorry, but if I could be what you wanted and what you needed, then I would." She looked up at him, her eyes brimming with unshed tears.

The tension left his body as he grabbed her waist and lifted her naked body to his. Her arms wound around his neck as she buried her face into his shoulder. She sighed as he placed kisses from her shoulder to the hollow of her neck and up to her cheek with ferocity. She turned her face to capture his mouth with her own, and they both moaned hungrily as the kiss deepened.

Roughly, Kaleb stepped forward to sandwich Zaria's body between his body and the wall as she dug her fingernails into his shoulders. He pressed urgent kisses filled with his desire and the energy of their argument against the top of her breasts. Undoing his pants, he jerked his boxers down until they fell to his knees.

Zaria gasped and arched her back as he grabbed her hips and slid her down onto his hardness with a thrust of his hips. The tears she held back broke, and Kaleb kissed them away as he stroked deep within her with an intensity fueled by every aspect of their emotions. "Yes . . . yes . . . yes," she cried out, gasping into his open mouth as she came with a power that shook her to her very core as she held on to him tightly, as if she would never feel him in her grasp again.

"I love you, Zaria," Kaleb moaned against her collarbone as his body stiffened and his thrusts became jerky as his seed filled her in many tiny explosions that visibly shook him.

His admission pained her.

She closed her eyes as her tears continued to fall and wet her cheeks and his shoulders. She held him closely and inhaled deeply of his scent, remembering everything about him. Storing it away to be remembered fondly some time in the future.

Zaria knew what they shared was memorable. In a different place and time in their lives, it could have been a great love story. But reality was never as great as the fairy tales.

"Good-bye, Kaleb," she whispered against his cheek before she moved to drop down to her feet.

He leaned back to look down at her. "Zaria—"

She shook her head and moved out of his grasp. "Good-bye," she said again softly.

Kaleb's eyes closed and his face hardened as he stepped back from her and jerked up his boxers and pants. "Humph. One last one for the road, huh?" he said sarcastically before he brushed past her and slammed out of the house.

Zaria winced and wrapped her arms around herself as the sound of that door slamming echoed around her.

Kaleb sat cloaked in total darkness is his living room, slumped in a club chair with his foot resting against the windowsill as he wished like hell that he'd never laid eyes on Zaria Ali. He stayed there in that chair long after the moon disappeared and the sun shone brightly. Even as he watched his ranch hands arriving through the gates of his ranch to begin a long day of work, he didn't move.

Kaleb had never been a man to wear his heart on his sleeve, and he foolishly proclaimed his love to Zaria—only to have her end things. To say good-bye forever. She was done with him.

And he was left with nothing but memories, regrets, and a broken heart.

His cell phone vibrated on the arm of his chair, and he shifted eyes that were red from lack of sleep to look at it. Kahron's number appeared. Kaleb shifted his eyes away and ignored the steady vibrating of the phone.

The only thing he could think of was wishing he could turn back time and never lay eyes on Zaria Ali.

Zaria clutched the pillow to her body and inhaled deeply of the scent of Kaleb that still clung to the cotton. It was damp with her tears from crying all night since he stormed out of her home. She missed him already. She ached for him. She had to fight not to call him.

It was time to let him go.

Zaria could never be the woman he wanted.

She just wished she had ended things sooner, before feelings were involved. His . . . and hers. She loved Kaleb Strong. She knew that now as the thought of living without him shook the very foundation she stood upon.

The days following the end of his relationship with Zaria, Kaleb was a hard taskmaster. He was relentless, pushing himself from the break of dawn to total darkness and expecting nothing less from his staff. It was the only way he knew to keep his mind off of Zaria.

He missed her. At times he hated her. He wanted to forget her.

Kaleb was sitting in his backyard in front of his lit fire pit when he heard the crunch of tires on the gravel of his front yard. He looked up as his brothers and father all climbed out of his father's diesel pickup truck and walked around the sizeable house toward the smoke they saw from the road.

"Thank God it's just a barrel," Kael said, shoving his hands into the pockets of his black Dickie jacket as his son grabbed folding chairs from the stack Kaleb kept by the rear patio deck.

The men surrounded the can, and Kaleb eyed them all with a heavy breath.

"What you doing, son?" Kael asked, unfolding his legs out before him to cross at the ankle.

Kaleb shrugged as he reached down into a cardboard box beside him and tossed something black and flimsy into the fire pit. "Just cleaning house," he said calmly.

Kael leaned over a bit to look down in the box. He frowned in disapproval. "It would have been more honorable to send the young lady her things and not roast them, son."

"Oh shit," one of his brothers swore.

Kaleb tugged his baseball cap down over his head before reaching into his box again. This time it was some scandalous book Zaria had left at his house. He lobbed that in as well.

Kael sighed as he reached down and picked up a stick long enough to use to pull the box over to him. "If you're done with her, be done with her stuff and send it to her."

Kaleb remained silent.

"Kade, do you remember back when you were in the eighth grade and you were in hot behind Roxanne Gregory?" Kael asked, looking over at his eldest and tallest boy.

Kade flung his head back and his laughter soon echoed into the cool air of the late September evening. "It took me three months to work up the nerve to ask her to the spring dance."

Kahron nodded and pointed at his oldest brother. "I remember that. Man, that was brutal when she turned you down in front of the whole cafeteria."

Kade shifted in his chair to eye Kahron. "No worse than Jennifer Thorn standing you up for your junior prom when she took Luke Freeman instead."

Kahron winced and did an exaggerated shiver. "Now *that* was cold. That was cold. Brrr."

"That was a tough suit you had on, though," Kaeden added, reaching over to give his brother some dap with a fist pound.

The men all laughed.

Kaleb eyed them with bored eyes. "Y'all were kids. I'm a grown-ass man and this ain't the same."

Kael eyed Kaleb as his laughter wound down. He leaned forward to press his elbows into his knees. "The point we're making—the point I want you to get, son—is we all have had our heart broke. But we're Strong men. We recover, we move on, and we use these good looks to find even better."

"I know that's right," Kahron added, smoothing his hands over his five o'clock shadow as he posed.

Kaleb shook his head and eyed the box now sitting beside his father. "Every last one of y'all leave tonight and you have these incredible women waiting for you. Me? I got a big-ass empty house and memories of making a fool out of myself."

Kael picked the box up and set it on the other side of him, closing it to hide the lacy lingerie he saw inside. "Boy, your mama broke my heart once and look where she at now," he boasted.

Kaleb and his brothers all looked over at their father in surprise.

"Ma?" they all said in unison.

Kael nodded and chuckled. "To make a long story short—and less embarrassing—your mama broke it off with me over a misunderstanding, and I had to fight like I never fought before to win her back. She put me through all kinds of tests and things to prove to her that I loved her, but I did it. She was worth it. And here we are, over thirty years later with a beautiful family and more happiness than I ever dreamed of having when I was in my twenties and still wet behind the ears."

"I never knew," Kade said, the fire dancing in his eyes as he glanced back to the flames.

"It was just me and your mama together for a long time before you came along, Kade. We have a lot of secrets and memories." Kael chuckled. "Lots of *good* times. Still have those good times."

Kaleb and his brothers all groaned. "Man, come on, Dad. Keep that to yourself," he said, making a face filled with distaste.

"You're missing the point, boy," Kael said, locking a hard glare on his son. "You either take your head out your ass and fight for this woman—"

"I don't want her," Kaleb insisted.

"Okay, fine, you don't want her. Then chuck it up to a loss and a lesson learned and move on with life. No more moping around or tearing your employees a new asshole. That ain't the way to run a business and you know it."

Kaleb shifted in his seat. "Who threw up the SOS?" he asked with a slight lift of the corner of his mouth—the closest thing to a smile he'd produced in almost a week.

"Don't worry about all that. Just remember what I taught all of you—"

"Treat your workers right and they'll do right by you," they all said in unison.

"Damn right."

Kaleb knew his father was right. He had taken all of his anger and frustration with Zaria out on his workers, men who worked for nearly a month with no pay when he first started out years ago. He knew a round of bonuses was in order.

A cell phone sounded and everyone reached for their devices.

"Hello," Kael eventually said, his deep and resonant voice even louder, as if he thought that whoever was on the other end of the phone couldn't hear him.

Kaeden stood up to walk over and stand by Kaleb, looking completely out of place in his three-piece striped suit. "You a'ight, man?" he asked, his deep-set eyes serious.

Kaleb nodded.

Kaeden reached out to grab Kaleb's strong shoulder to squeeze and then pat twice before he walked back to his seat. The show of support and concern made Kaleb smile. Of all the brothers, who would have thought that Kaeden, considered the weakest when they were growing up because of his allergies to everything under the sun, would feel the need to check on his older and supposedly stronger brother?

Zaria didn't love him, but Kaleb knew that he was loved by his family and that was just as important.

Kael stood up and walked over to the truck, still talking loudly on his phone. The brothers all eyed each other when he began to swear, and they heard their sister's name several times during the tirade.

"I wonder what stunt Kat pulled this time," Kahron said, folding his hands in the air between his knees.

Kade shook his head and smiled, his deep dimples showing. "I think she's responsible for some of these gray hairs we *all* have."

Kaeden reached into the inside pocket of his blazer and took out his inhaler, shaking it vigorously. "We should own stock in Gucci. That's for sure," he said before taking a deep toke from his inhaler.

Kaleb laughed. "It's going to take something drastic to get her to look at life a little different. We all spoiled her, even when Ma told us not to."

"True, true," Kahron agreed.

The men fell silent and Kaleb had to admit that he was glad for the presence of his family—the camaraderie of his father and his brothers. He was still aching for everything that would never be with Zaria—that hadn't changed and wouldn't for a minute—but he felt a little better. He was reminded that he was a Strong and the Strongs faced adversity head-on and came out even stronger on the other side.

"Zaria, I need two rum and Cokes, please."

Zaria looked over at the waitress and nodded to let her know she got the order. She worked her ankles in her new sequined flats before finishing up a piña colada to set before her customer. She collected their money, made change, accepted their generous tip, and started on the two rum and Cokes.

She pushed her hair out of her face and focused on the task at hand. She was moving on autopilot. Her focus? To get through her shift and then she was determined to have a night out. She was determined to get back in her glory, remembering the days she would hit up different clubs every night from Wednesday to Sunday. There was always a club popping somewhere in or around Charleston.

Zaria turned to grab her cloth to wipe down the bar and a flash of silver caught her eye. It reminded her of the first night she'd laid eyes on Kaleb, especially when she looked up in the mirror and saw him standing there behind her in the reflection.

It felt like déjà vu.

She blinked and looked again. He wasn't there. She turned and her eyes scanned the crowd for him, but she knew it was nothing more than a vision of Kaleb mocking her and the decision she had to live with.

A wave of sadness washed over her, and she literally shook it off.

She hadn't seen or spoken to him since that night. Even though she half expected him to come rushing back into the house to demand more from her, in time she realized that he was not coming back. It was over. Their time had finally run its course . . . or he *had* finally found the woman he wanted to try and build a future with. Either way, she knew his life didn't include her anymore. It couldn't.

Another woman would swell with his child and be blessed with his kisses. Another woman would share his life.

Zaria would become nothing more than a footnote in his young life.

She counted the minutes until her shift was over and then—

"Zaria?"

She froze at the sound of her ex-husband's voice.

"Zaria," he said again.

Giving herself a five count that wasn't nearly enough before she turned to find not only her ex but also his new wife at his side. *Great . . . just damn great.*

"Ned," she said shortly, not even acknowledging the woman who stole him from her, especially when the wench wrapped her arm around him in a decidedly possessive move.

Zaria eyed them, trying to decide if she should follow her gut and go to the left and pull on her big-girl panties and do what's right. "You know, Barbie," she said, "you don't have to be worried that Ned will ever get to do the divorcée double back with me, because you see, little girl, tricks are for kids and *that* trick is all yours." Zaria smiled at her, pointing to Ned.

"Oops," said the man sitting at the bar next to where Ned stood.

Not done yet, Zaria pushed some napkins toward her ex. "You better mop up some of that dye juice turning your shirt collar black," she said.

That brought out a full chuckle from the man and a few others within earshot.

"Why you have to be so immature and disrespectful?" Ned asked, his jaw clenching.

Zaria sighed and studied the white tips of her acrylic nails before she cut cold eyes at him. "Immaturity is fun sometimes, and I like to have fun.

Now, *disrespectful* was you coming in here to speak to me, bringing along the woman with whom you cheated on me. *That's* disrespectful. What you should have done was act like you didn't even see me and take your new baby bride, get her a high chair, and go sit your ass down. You definitely shouldn't drag her up in my face. Clear?"

"Umph, umph umph," the customer said, openly staring.

Ned frowned at the man before he grabbed his wife's arm and turned to walk away.

Zaria rolled her eyes so hard she was glad they didn't get stuck. "Sucka mother—"

"Shut you mouth," the customer teased, pointing at her with a big toothy grin.

Zaria laughed, reaching out to swat his hand playfully before moving down to the other end of the bar.

After fixing a few more drinks and cleaning her area, Zaria let her manager know she was taking a break. She headed for the restroom, crossing the foyer and thinking of the night she had first crossed paths with Kaleb. She smiled a bit at the time they'd shared. It hadn't ended well, but she didn't regret having Kaleb in her life for even such a brief time. He was a remarkable man who'd treated her well and shared some moments of her life that the next man would find damn hard to equal or top.

She missed him.

She craved him.

She loved him.

Setting him free had been the hardest thing she'd ever had to do in her life.

As she felt tears well up yet again, she rushed into the bathroom and into one of the stalls, taking a seat on the closed lid of the commode.

If she had ever thought of getting married again and having more children, she would have gladly set aside their age difference and been the woman Kaleb was looking for. Of course, he would always be chasing her by more than a decade in age, but Zaria knew that if she hadn't been so wounded by her divorce, she could have easily been "the one" for Kaleb. Easily.

Needing a distraction, she pulled her cell phone from the deep pocket of her slacks and called her twins. "Hey, Ma," Meena said. "I'm putting you on speaker."

"Hey, Ma!" Neema said.

"What y'all doing?" she asked, forcing the sadness and the hint of tears from her voice.

"We just came back from buying our books for school," she said.

"Need any money?" she asked.

"No, Daddy sent it," Neema said, with her slight lisp.

Zaria was proud of her will not to clue her kids in to just how much she detested their father. That she wouldn't do because it didn't benefit them to be hurt and stressed. "Good, that's good."

"Something wrong, Ma?" Meena asked, sounding like she was smacking on something.

"Just wanted to talk to my girls and let you know how much I love y'all and miss you and I'm proud of you," she said softly, closing her eyes as she remembered the day she first brought them home.

"We love you too."

"You should come see us. We got the furniture for our apartment. It looks good," Neema said.

Zaria sat up straighter. "Maybe I will," she said, wanting to see her girls.

"Good. But, Ma, no clubbing or hanging out on campus this time. We just want our mom, you know?" Meena asked, her voice soft and a little hesitant like she worried about hurting Zaria's feelings.

Zaria frowned. "I was just having fun, and your friends liked me."

"Yes, and you were the talk of the campus for weeks after that, Ma," Neema drawled. "It's not fun having boys talking about how good your mama drops it like it's hot. O-kay?"

"O-kay!" Meena agreed.

"You were voted MILF of the year last semester."

"MILF?" Zaria asked.

One of the twins sighed—she couldn't tell which one.

"Ma, MILF stands for 'mother I'd like to . . .'"

"Like to what?" Zaria asked.

One of the twins whispered the term.

Zaria gasped in shock at first and then arched her brow. "I was?"

"Ma!" they both exclaimed.

Zaria bit her bottom lip as she heard the commode in the stall next to her flush. "I guess that is embarrassing."

"Completely," Meena said.

At the thought of spending time with her daughters, Zaria felt her spirits brighten a little bit. It would be a nice distraction from the heartache that took her completely by surprise when falling in love again wasn't even penciled on her agenda.

I love you, Zaria.

Her heart literally ached as she remembered his admission of love. She'd never wanted to break his heart.

As long as you both are on the same page.

Guilt filled her because she should have heeded his mother's gentle warning.

"You're not bringing your newest boy toy, are you, because we want you to stay here with us," Neema said.

"No, no boy toys. Just me and my girls," she promised.

"Good," they both said.

CHAPTER 10

One month later

Kaleb was determined to get his ish together.

His relationship with his crew was back on target. The lightening of his dark mood plus a nice bonus in their weekly paycheck had shown the men his apologies. They still worked hard but now it was back to feeling like a sport instead of a chore.

His business was booming, and he started making plans to actually sell some of his own dairy products in a small store he wanted to open on the ranch. Plenty of dairy farmers did it, but now he felt he was ready to tackle yet another aspect of his business.

He was back with the rest of his family at Holtsville Baptist Church and was spending the afternoons with them, enjoying good food and a great family.

He thought of Zaria one less moment as each day passed until he knew eventually she would mean no more to him than any of his other exes. At least he hoped so. He still loved her, but he was resigned to the fact that they weren't meant to be and it was more than just their age difference.

Kaleb looked at the brick town house as he pulled into the driveway behind a charcoal-gray two-door Miata with the license tag LEGAL. The sun was just starting to fade as he left his SUV and made his way up the few steps to the black front door to knock. He felt a little nervous but flexed his shoulders in the dark denims he wore with an oatmeal suede blazer and crisp white cotton shirt.

The door opened and Heather appeared, stepping back behind the door as she opened it wider. "Hi, Kaleb," she said with a soft dimpled smile. Her petite figure looked pretty in a deep peach, soft cashmere wrap dress.

He bent down to press a kiss to her cheek before stepping inside her home for the first time. It suited her, with soft and feminine touches in muted tones that made her home warm. *No fuchsia or gold or leopard prints.*

"I was very surprised when you called me yesterday," she said, folding her small but curvaceous frame onto the sofa. "I thought you threw my number away."

Kaleb took a seat on the other end of the sofa, unbuttoning his blazer first. "Actually I did, since I was seeing someone, but that didn't work out. But I remember you and remembered your name and looked you up," he admitted, crossing his ankle over his knee.

"Thank goodness for phonebooks and such," she said with a little laugh that seemed restrained.

Nothing at all like Zaria when she flung her head back and laughed freely until she cried and clutched her belly.

Stop it, Kaleb.

He looked around her home and spotted a small piano in the corner just off the large front bay windows.

She followed his gaze and then stood. "Actually, I wanted to play a little something for you before we went to dinner," she said, easing past his legs and her glass coffee table to move over to the piano to take a seat on the bench.

He turned on his seat to face her as she began to play a smooth jazzy beat that he soon recognized as a Miles Davis tune. He was impressed by her skill. She handled the keys with power and authority, still able to bring forth sweet and haunting tunes.

But as he placed his head in his hand and closed his eyes to take in the music, all he could see was an image of Zaria in her short gold skirt and heels, fidgeting in her seat and eventually falling asleep on his shoulder and snoring just as loudly as a man. What had irked his nerves then made him smile now.

When he finally opened his eyes, Heather had stopped playing and was watching him with a twinkle in her eye. "Are you sleeping?" she asked playfully.

"Nooo, no. That was excellent," he said, rising to his feet. "I was just remembering something from the past."

"Who introduced a dairy farmer to jazz?" she

asked, moving over to collect her coat to hand to him.

"My dad," he said, holding her coat for her.

Heather touched his hand as she looked over her shoulder up at him. "Maybe I'll get to play for him sometime," she offered.

"Actually, I thought maybe we could have dinner at my parents'. If that's cool with you," he offered, making a last-minute decision.

"That's more than fine," Heather said as they walked out the door. "I bet your mama can cook too."

Kaleb held her elbow lightly as they descended the few steps. "Sure can," he said with a huge smile.

He helped her into the passenger seat of his SUV.

"And don't you worry—parents always love me," she said with a wink.

Kaleb shut the door and came around to climb into the driver's seat. He turned his satellite radio to a jazz station and pointed the SUV toward Holtsville. A slight drizzle began to fall, and the combination of the cozy interior and the sultry music lulled them into a comfortable zone. They talked a little. They laughed a little. They shared things about each other.

But truthfully, in the back of his mind, although Heather said all the right things and seemed to be just what he needed for his happily-ever-after, his thoughts were filled with Zaria. He was unfairly comparing the two women.

Kaleb knew he was wrong.

He was grateful when he finally turned the SUV off the main highway onto the long and curving asphalt road. He saw Heather looking intently out the window at the sizeable brick two-story structure with dozens of clear glass-paned windows. The manicured lawns. The freshly painted shutters and flower boxes. It was a beautiful and stately home, and he was proud of his parents' accomplishments.

Kaleb parked in front of the house in the row of cars belonging to his family. "Don't be nervous," he said, knowing his clan could be overwhelming. Kaleb wondered if he'd made the right choice in bringing her.

"I'm not," she said with perky confidence.

Shrugging, he jogged up the stairs beside her and then stepped forward to push the door open. His parents rarely ever locked the front door.

The raucous noise of family reached them as Kaleb hung up Heather's coat and escorted her to the family room, where the entire clan was watching his niece Kadina and his sister-in-law Garcelle playing a dancing game on the Wii system.

Everyone waved, almost distractedly, as they focused back on Kadina and Garcelle, who eventually made a wrong move and lost. Still the stepmother and stepdaughter team laughed good-naturedly as they gave each other a high five.

Kaleb led Heather around the room and made speedy introductions. Everyone greeted her warmly, and he could see their curiosity about her. It wasn't long before his father and brothers rose to corner him, while his mother patted the seat on the sofa next to her.

Kael shoved his hands into his pockets and rocked back and forth on his heels as he eyed his son.

Kade crossed his arms over his chest and looked down at Kaleb in disbelief.

Kahron chuckled.

Kaeden rattled his inhaler in his pocket like most men rattled change.

Kaleb held his hands out. "What?" he asked.

"Boy, where in the devil did you dig that girl up from?" Kael asked.

"Oh, man, come on. Y'all acting like I went to an escort service. Like I can't get a woman. Come on, dude, don't play me," he spouted.

"So you're over Zaria?" Kade asked, almost like a second father to all of his younger brothers.

"Excuse me, but I don't think it's polite to be in a huddle talking about a woman while I have another here with me," Kaleb said, easing his strong and broad figure through Kade and Kahron to head into the kitchen.

Garcelle and Bianca were taking heaping dishes from the kitchen into the dining room. "*Hola*, Kaleb," Garcelle said before disappearing with a bowl of steamed cabbage.

Bianca gave him a nod, her hands full with a platter of fried catfish and homemade corn bread. His stomach growled as he moved over to the fridge to look inside, more for habit's sake than really wanting anything.

When the kitchen door swung open, he turned to find his mother standing in the kitchen watching him closely. "I am starving, Ma. The fish looks good," he said.

"Kaleb Alexander Strong, why did you bring

that poor woman here?" she asked him, coming around the island to lean back against it and look up at her son.

"What do you mean, Ma?" he asked, turning again to open the fridge as a clear diversion.

Lisha began to snap her fingers. "What is it gay men call women they use to hide that they're gay? What is it?" she asked, tapping her chin as she looked up at the ceiling.

Kaleb closed the fridge and turned to face her. "A beard."

Lisha snapped her fingers soundly one last time. "That's right. A beard. Kaleb, that woman is your . . . your . . ."

"Ma, you know I'm not gay," he drawled.

"But you are pretending to be something you're not . . . and to your family," she finished softly in disapproval.

Kaleb shifted where he stood.

"Any fool can see that you still care for Zaria, regardless of whether you'll be together. Your heart is full and until it's empty—or at least emptier—you don't have room in it for someone else . . . especially a woman like Heather who is ready to settle down, baby."

Kaleb frowned deeply.

"When it comes to matters of the heart—yours and others—you have to be fair or karma can and will bite you deep in the ass, Kaleb," Lisha warned.

Kaleb nodded in understanding, welcoming his mother's wisdom and the kiss she pressed to his cheek.

* * *

Zaria was done moping.

Any spare time not spent with her daughters or working, she spent thinking about Kaleb. Wondering if he was back on the prowl and imagining him with a dozen faceless women who would be more than happy to claim the spot of his woman. And again, just like the weeks after her divorce, her life was on hold.

She hadn't been on a date.

She spent her days off in the house draped in dreary sweats and flipping through cable channels.

She hadn't even gotten a number to add to her drawer.

Nothing.

Her life was on definite pause, and Zaria was ready to push PLAY.

She checked her appearance in the mirror, loving her fitted jeans and thigh-high boots she wore with a faux fur over her turtleneck. She added a few rhinestone bracelets and a long chain with an amulet before she grabbed an oversized black bag with lots of metal buckles and headed out the door. October in South Carolina didn't bring on the chill like the eastern states, but it wasn't exactly Florida either when the sun wasn't shining high in the sky. As soon as it dipped, so did the temperature. Zaria felt chilled to the bone as she rushed out to her car and hurried inside. She slid in a Best of the '80s old-school rap CD that reminded her of her high school years and headed out.

She moved in her seat as she listened to the hits by the Fat Boys, Loe Moe Dee, Roxanne Shanté, MC Shan, Big Daddy, Slick Rick, Doug E. Fresh, and Biz Markie. By the time she reached her destination, she was in a definite party mood, parking her car outside the club. Looking for the cars of the coworkers she was supposed to meet there, she used her cell to call them.

"Lashaunda? Where y'all at?" she asked.

"Turning into the parking lot right now."

"A'ight." Zaria flipped the phone closed and climbed out of her VW, holding the straps of her pocketbook on the bend of her elbow as she locked her car. Turning, she spotted Lashaunda's Chevy Caprice with the colorful Frosted Flakes car wrap and rims that had the car riding higher than most other vehicles on the road.

She walked over to her coworkers carefully, as the dirt-packed yard had random rocks. Lashaunda and Peaches were just climbing out of the car in matching velour bodysuits and thigh-high boots that only reached just below their knees because both were heavily built. *Lawd,* Zaria thought, giving Peaches' three rolls around her middle a definite side-eye.

Zaria was thick on the bottom herself, and she held no discrimination against a plus-sized beauty who knew how to snatch everything together with style like Mo'Nique, but pushing everything into a catsuit with no sign of a girdle was dicey at best.

"This club be off the chain, Ms. Zaria," Peaches said, flashing two diamond-studded gold teeth.

As soon as they paid their fee, Zaria left them behind to hit the dance floor at the sound of a reggae joint blaring against the walls. When she felt a hand at her waist, Zaria looked over her shoulder but frowned at the skinny braided young man dancing with her. He looked to be no more than eighteen. Zaria liked to date younger men but not those young enough to still be babysat. She turned and danced back from him, putting distance between them big enough for two more people to fit in.

He lifted a blunt to his lip, the lit end flashing in the dimly lit club, before he released a stream of thick gray smoke heavy enough to set off a fire alarm—if the club had one. That made her rise up on the tips of her high-heeled boots to look for a rear entrance. That was lacking too.

She kept coughing and pretending to gag and eventually the baby gangsta was dancing away from her, his braids swinging back and forth across his dingy racing jacket. As Zaria continued to dance and really took a good look at her surroundings, she saw nothing but younger men in sneakers and oversized jeans. It was a toss-up on which side of the law they dwelled. Smoke filled the air, making everything two feet below the ceiling look like Los Angeles smog.

"All you fine bitches who want a nigga to beat that thang up, hit the floor right now, ho!"

Zaria's mouth fell open in pure shock at the disrespect, but what shocked her even more were the young women flocking to fill the dance floor—including Peaches and Lashaunda! The lyrics to the song that blasted made her stop dancing, and she got jostled about in the crowd as more profanity than real lyrics filled the air.

Zaria took a deep breath and then regretted it because she just knew she had inhaled some of the weed smoke in the air. Surrounded by pure foolishness, the music faded for her and she felt like she was in the middle of a distorted dream as she had one of those "aha" moments Oprah seemed to cherish.

She felt alone. More alone and lost than she ever had in her life.

She felt out of place. Like a gay man at a female strip club.

She missed Kaleb. Missed him and wanted him and loved him.

She felt like the club was getting smaller or more people had packed in as the crowd seemed to swell in on her. She wouldn't want her children partying at a spot like this. *So why am I?*

She looked for the girls to throw up a deuce before she left, but she didn't see them and she was ready to go. *Hell with it. They ain't riding with me.*

Zaria worked her way through the crowd, ignoring all the young men pulling at her.

Pow-pow-pow.

The music screeched to a halt, and all hell broke loose at the sound of gunfire. As Zaria felt her body being pushed forward with the crowd as everyone tried to fit through the one door in the joint, she crossed her fingers and prayed like she *never* prayed before. Out loud and proud!

"Oh God, if you can hear me over this foolishness, *pleeeeeease* get me safely to my car so that I can take my black behind home and be in church *early* Sunday morning and pay my tithes," she prayed at the top of her voice over the screams and commotion.

She felt the heat of the bodies. Feet pressed down on hers as some men pushed women out of the way. Body odors she preferred not to inhale nearly choked her. She could have sworn she felt tugging on her bag like someone's hand was in it. She jerked her bag forward as hard as she could and heard two cries. One from behind—the pickpocket—and one from the girl in front of her she accidentally rammed the bag into.

Zaria shook her head as her heart beat faster than a racehorse reaching the final stretch. "And, God, please, guide me out of this mess. *Lawd please,*" she wailed, drawing the odd stares of people near her.

She could hear police sirens, and she honestly didn't know if they were going to make it better or worse. All she did know was it was just like her third strike in a baseball game and she was O-U-T!

She saw the door ahead and started pushing with the rest of the crowd. As she neared the door, she got jammed between someone's body and the door frame until another push from the crowd made her burst out the door and fall to the ground. Zaria rolled out of the way and then scrambled to her feet, feeling every rock and pebble that had pressed into her body. She took a deep breath and started to run for her vehicle as the tires of people racing away squealed against the road. It took a minute for her to realize the heel of her boot was gone, giving her a lopsided Hunchback of Notre Dame run.

Just before she made it inside her car, she saw Lashaunda and Peaches headed toward where they parked. The dips and dimples of their behinds jiggling in a thousand different directions. Zaria pointed her fingers to the heavens in thanks, started her car with shaking hands, and reversed out of the parking lot, almost into oncoming traffic. Almost.

Zaria didn't settle down until she was almost home. "Whooo," she sighed, shaking her head.

She thought about that last argument she had had with Kaleb and his condemnation of her partying ways. She could only imagine what he would say if he knew about her night.

Zaria was still feeling nervous anxiety when she finally pulled into her yard. She was surprised to see her daughters' joint vehicle parked there. As she left her VW, she fought the urge to crawl up the stairs and into the house because her legs were as wobbly as Jell-O.

Both the girls were sitting on the sofa when she entered the house. They both looked at her with wide eyes. "What happened to you?" Meena asked.

Zaria glanced at her reflection in the mirror by the front door. Her hair was disheveled. Her black clothes dusty and dirty. Her once-fluffy faux fur looked more like roadkill. Her makeup smudged and destroyed by the sweat that poured off her from the heat of bodies. "I had to change a flat. Long story. I'm home safe. End of story," she said, setting her keys and bag on the wooden end table as she hobbled past on her destroyed boots.

"Oh my God, there was a shooting at Club Nine-eleven," Meena said.

Zaria froze and looked over her shoulder as her daughter used the remote to turn up the newscast.

Sure enough, a picture of the death trap she had escaped was on the screen.

Neema looked up and saw Zaria still standing there. "We came home to go to that club tonight," she said, tucking her feet beneath her the way Zaria always did.

Meena nodded in agreement. "Good thing we didn't go, huh?" she asked, glancing at her mother. "They keep something going on at that club."

The fact that her children had more sense to steer clear of the foolishness made Zaria feel all the more idiotic for being there. "Thank God my babies got good sense to steer clear of trouble," Zaria said as a spasm radiated across her back and made her wince.

"You sure you all right, Mama?" Neema asked.

Zaria just nodded and waved her hand before walking into her bedroom and closing the door securely behind her. She barely peeled off her boots and chucked her flat fur across the room before she dropped onto the bed. She hugged one of her many pillows close to her.

You actually believe everything you do is some show of liberation and claiming yourself and all that crap, when all you're tying to do is prove to him that you could have been what he wanted.

Was Kaleb right?

Her life had flashed before her in that death trap.

She couldn't let her legacy end with a life of trying to party away the pain of her divorce. There had to be another way.

Zaria felt herself drifting to sleep, and she slid her hand inside her pillow and pressed her fingertips to the photo of Kaleb she kept there just before her soft snores filled the air.

The next night, Zaria and her daughters walked into Oscar's Restaurant in Summerville. As soon as they were seated at one of the booths, their waiter, a tall bald-headed brothah with long lashes, appeared at the table and they ordered sweet tea and their favorite appetizers of crab cakes on fried green tomatoes.

"It's been a while since we all went out to eat," Meena said, already reaching for the sweet butter and basket of rolls on the table.

"Yes, this is nice," Zaria agreed, looking across at her twin girls who shared the seat across from her.

"I don't need a menu. I already know what I want," Neema said.

The three ladies eyed each other before saying in unison, "Short ribs."

They all laughed.

Zaria licked her lips before she eyed them again. "I know you girls hated the new Zaria. It's just that the divorce from your father kinda knocked me a little bit and, um . . . I did what made me feel better."

They looked at her.

"I'm not going to say that I will give up going to an occasional party here and there, but, um, I'm definitely cutting back some," she admitted to them, taking a deep sip of her sweet tea.

They shared a look. "Is this because of Kaleb?" Neema asked.

Zaria arched a brow. "Kaleb and I are no more," she said, her heart feeling like it was pierced with a knife.

Meena shrugged. "When you cut out all the partying when you were with him and seemed so happy and all of that, we kinda thought maybe he wasn't that bad for you."

"It's nice seeing you happy—not just having fun but really being happy," Neema added.

Zaria looked at them in surprise. "He *was* good for me, but I wasn't the right woman for him. So I ended it. It was my decision."

They shared another look. "We're not trying to get all in your business or nothing. It was just nice seeing you happy, and now you look sad a lot, that's all."

Zaria reached across the table and cupped one of their hands with each of her own. "I really liked him but sometimes like—"

"Love," they corrected her in unison.

Zaria smiled. "Sometimes *it's* not enough."

"Like you and Daddy?" Neema asked.

Zaria just forced a stiff smile and nodded. *Bless their hearts. They have no clue just how much of a dog their father truly is.*

Thankfully the waiter came with their appetizers and the girls' attention switched from her tortured love life to their appetizers.

Zaria's thoughts were filled as she pushed her crab cake around on the plate, not really hungry. Mostly she wanted to spend time with her daughters. She was glad that their relationship had made a smooth transition from mother-daughter to a blend of motherhood and friendship.

Thankfully she was the one who went through the growing pains instead of them.

Two hours later, Zaria watched both of her daughters sit back against their booth and hold a hand to their flat guts. They were truly identical.

"I am so full," they both said before sharing a look and laughing.

Their waiter, dressed in all black, began to clear their empty dishes. "Any dessert for you ladies?" he asked, his eyes lingering on Meena just a bit longer.

Zaria watched as Meena gave him a long look in return.

"None for me," Zaria said, rising to her feet. "I'm headed to the ladies' room."

He offered directions, but Zaria waved him off, knowing the way. She relieved herself quickly and then left the stall to wash her hands and splash water on her face. She felt achy in her joints, especially her ankles and her lower back. She knew her days bartending for eight- to ten-hour shifts at a time might be coming to an end. The idea of a simpler way to make money sounded appealing.

She made her way back to the table and pushed cash into the black leather billfold awaiting her. The table was empty. "Your daughters are waiting for you outside," their waiter said politely.

Zaria nodded. "Thank you. We had a good time as always," she told him. "Keep the change."

"Yes, ma'am," he said. "You have a good night."

Zaria was digging in her purse as she walked into the waiting area. She looked up just as Kaleb and the cutie from outside the club—the attorney—were led into the dining room. He turned and looked back at her over his shoulder.

Zaria knuckled up and gave him a short wave before turning and rushing out the door before one tear had a chance to fall.

Kaleb appeared to be studying his menu but truly his mind was on Zaria. Although she had no right to question or judge him, he knew what she had to be thinking of him at that moment. He hated the thought of that because even though she never asked for exclusivity, Kaleb had given nothing less.

And he saw the look of surprise and hurt in her eyes before she tossed him that fake wave and left.

"I don't think she's too happy about seeing us together," Heather said, closing her own menu and gently setting it down on the table.

Kaleb shifted his eyes up to look at her. "I didn't think you saw her."

Heather nodded. "She's really tall and pretty and hard to miss," she said.

Yes, yes she is, he thought to himself.

"Nice restaurant," Heather said, looking around. "I've never been here before."

Kaleb nodded. "We come and watch sporting events in the bar sometimes," he told her, his thoughts still elsewhere.

Any fool can see that you still care for Zaria, regard-

less of whether you'll be together or not. Your heart is full and until it's empty—or at least emptier—you don't have room in it for someone else. . . .

After seeing Zaria, he knew his mother had hit the nail on the head regarding his feelings for her.

"You know, if seeing her has put a damper on the evening, I'd rather we call it an early night and come back another time," she suggested.

"I'm sorry," Kaleb said. "I didn't mean to ruin the evening. It's not like I'd rather she be sitting here, because we didn't work out. It's just that—"

"You don't want to go back but you're not ready to move on. Not yet, right?" she said.

Kaleb struggled for words and could find nothing but the truth. "I'm sorry," he told her honestly.

"I'd rather you tell me now than later," she told him.

As they gathered their things and left the restaurant, Kaleb knew he had done the right thing by being honest with Heather.

When it comes to matters of the heart—yours and others—you have to be fair or karma can and will bite you deep in the ass, Kaleb. . . .

He was doing bad enough in the love department without karma adding fuel to the explosion.

Chapter 11

Zaria loved her daughters and enjoyed their company, but the last thing she wanted was for them to see her fall completely to pieces. And that's what she did as soon as she was alone. As soon as the front door shut behind them and they carried their laughter and their light with them, she crumbled to the floor and wept like a baby. Long after the sun faded from the sky and a chill filled the house, Zaria remained there, feeling lost and alone until she shivered from the cold and forced herself up to drag to bed.

She pulled the covers over her head and balled her body into a tight knot, wishing that when she closed her eyes, she didn't see images of the man she loved with another woman—especially that particular woman.

Zaria didn't know her and couldn't care less about her, but the younger and smarter woman who shared things in common with Kaleb obviously had made an impact on him. She was the one he ran to for comfort after she broke his heart.

I love you, Zaria. I love you.

She was filled with regrets. As he made love to her with a fierceness like nothing she had ever known, Zaria wished with everything inside of her that she could have just told him the truth. She wished she could have just let her emotions slip from her tongue and let the chips fall where they may.

But she was too old to even think of having children, and starting a family was so important to him. How could they overlook such a huge obstacle *and* the fact that she didn't want to remarry?

The next morning, she forced herself out of bed, determined to get on with life and to make some changes for the better. Her better.

Kaleb was finding his forever after she'd turned him down. She shed her tears, she still carried around the numbness, but she had to move on with life.

Just like everyone else around her.

Her best friends were happily in love.

The man she loved had found someone new.

Even her ex-husband was happily wed to another.

Maybe she *had* taken on a younger persona to be everything she thought he wanted in a woman . . . like Kaleb said. And the thought of any truth in that type of subconscious crap on her behalf didn't rest well on her shoulders.

It was time to figure out why she couldn't get her act in gear—and she knew just where to start. She grabbed her phone and made a few calls, feeling a bit more satisfied when she was done.

After a long and hot shower, Zaria took her time to get dressed. She applied her makeup, slid on an all-winter white ensemble of a V-neck sweater dress that clung to her curves, nude suede boots that gave her a few more inches of height, and an ivory wool trench coat that finished it off nicely.

Zaria left the house with her head held high and climbed into her car. She dug out the sheet of notepad paper with directions on it and steered her car toward Beaufort.

It took forty-five minutes and way too much time reflecting on some of her actions after her divorce before she finally parked on the street in front of a pretty blue and white Cape Cod–style house.

For a minute she sat with her eyes locked on the matching blue and white business sign in the front yard.

JULIA DENNISON, PHD
THE FIRST STEP TO YOUR WELL-BEING

Self-discovery wasn't fun or easy, but most times it was very necessary. Zaria climbed from the car, and walked up the short walkway to the front door, shivering a bit from the slight chill in the air. The wooden sign said OPEN and Zaria turned the knob and stepped inside.

The house had been turned into a true office. What was once a living room was now a waiting room with a glass-enclosed receptionist station. It was empty.

A door opened and a petite woman in her

early sixties with a low-cut Afro, a bright smile, and deep dimples stepped back to allow Zaria to enter. "Zaria?" she asked.

"Yes."

"Come on back."

Zaria nodded as she worked her clutch in her hands as she stepped into the back offices. "Thank you for agreeing to see me today," she said over her shoulder.

"First open door on the left," the woman said from behind her.

Zaria felt nervous as she stepped into a sizeable office complete with bookshelves and African artwork. The muted gold on the walls and the dark wood of the furnishings made her feel comfortable as she took a seat on the leather love seat, crossing her legs.

She watched the woman pick up a notepad and pen and slide glasses onto her face before taking a seat across from Zaria in an oversized club chair that seemed to dwarf her. "I am Dr. Dennison," she said. "I am very happy that you are here and that you came on your own, because it means you are open to the process. You are free to find balance in your life. You are welcome to peace of mind," she began. "Now, do you have any questions for me?"

Zaria felt herself relax. Something about the woman made her feel at home. "No . . . no, I don't."

She nodded. "Then I have one for you, Zaria. Why are you here?"

Zaria licked her lips and looked down at her hands before looking back up at her. "I have been in love twice in my whole life. The first time my husband left me for another woman and the second time I left the man I love because he was younger than me. Both breakups have really messed me up, and I can admit that. I need help getting through them."

"And do you believe that your husband's treatment of your marriage plays a role in you ending the second relationship?"

Zaria was surprised when tears welled up. "Now? Yes, I do."

"Tell me about the days after your husband decided to leave."

And Zaria did. With total honesty she replayed it all. Her anger. Her hurt. Her pain. Her confusion. Her shock.

Her insecurities.

"How do you feel about your ex-husband?" she asked.

Zaria's gut clenched. "I hate him. I am annoyed by him. Every chance I get I take pleasure in insulting him," she said with total disclosure.

Dr. Dennison nodded. "I can see your rage. I can feel it."

"So can I, Doc, so can I," Zaria assured her.

Dr. Dennison smiled a bit. "Were you happy in the marriage? Was it everything you wanted it to be socially, financially, psychologically, and sexually?"

"I would have stayed married if he hadn't cheated and left," Zaria said.

Dr. Dennison shook her head. "No, no, no, Zaria. Were you happy?" she asked again, motioning with her slender finger.

Zaria leaned back against the plushness of the love seat and replayed her marriage in her head. "No. No, I wasn't happy," she admitted.

"And are you happier now?"

"Yes," Zaria said instantly.

"Sounds like he did you a favor moving on," Dr. Dennison said. "Can you see past his untruths, his adultery, his crap—because that is what it is. Those are *his* issues. They affected you but all of that is his mess that he has to deal with. Can you see how him taking all of his mess and leaving you free to be out of an unhappy marriage actually did you a favor?"

Zaria shook her head as she crossed her legs and rocked her foot like she wanted to free it from her ankle. "When it comes to him, all I see is the betrayal—and me leaving my size-ten shoe dead in his ass, Doc. I want to implant my foot there and leave it for him to walk around with for the rest of his days."

The doctor swallowed back a smile. "Okay, we have to slow walk this I see, because until you release some of that anger for him, you can't move on from it and release yourself."

"You're good, Doc," Zaria admitted, dropping her head back on the couch.

"And we've only just begun," she assured her.

As soon as Zaria left Beaufort after her fifty-minute session with Dr. Dennison, she steered her car toward Walterboro for her next appointment. She parked her car and strolled into the restaurant, eventually claiming the seat the hostess led her to in the back. Not more than five minutes later, Ned strolled in dressed in a suit with his overcoat slung over his arm.

It was different from his usual uniform attire, and Zaria could even admit that her ex-husband was still a fine-looking man as he strolled toward her.

"You're mighty spiffy, Ned," she said, her legs crossed as she leaned back comfortably in her chair.

"We had church this morning," he said before taking his seat.

"On a Saturday?"

"We're Seventh-Day Adventist," he said impatiently.

Zaria chuckled. "Okay. When we were married, you were No Day Nothing because you never went to church."

"What is this all about, Zaria?"

"When I first called you, my intention was to cuss you out, to let you know how much I hated you and wanted to see you hurt like you hurt me," she began. "But I'm seeing things a little different now, and although I'm not a hundred percent sold on this, I am willing to accept things for what they are."

Ned watched her and said nothing.

"For years I let what you did to me affect my life more than I like to admit," she said. "I was just as unhappy as you were in our marriage, and although I hate the way you handled it, at least you were willing to claim your happiness . . . you know? If you hadn't left me, I would have stayed married to you, stayed having this okay sex—"

Ned's face stiffened.

Zaria held up her hands. "Hear me out. *Neither* one of us were happy. Okay? I didn't have the balls to leave, and when you left me, it shattered everything I thought I knew about myself. And even though it hurt—and it did hurt, Ned—we weren't supposed to be together anymore."

Ned continued to watch her closely like he didn't trust her next move.

"I wish you had handled things different, but I can say now that you leaving me was the best thing you could have done for me, so why should I hate you and be mad when you opened up the opportunity for me to enjoy the second half of my life more than I did the first half."

A waitress came up to their table, but Zaria waved her away as she rose to her feet. "I want you to know that I forgive you, Ned. I forgive you and I thank you for being a good dad to my girls—"

"*Our* girls," he stressed, correcting her.

Zaria nodded as she tucked her neutral alligator-print clutch under her arm. "You're right. Our girls. They are the best things to ever happen to me—no, to us."

He nodded. "I agree."

"It's time we get past the petty arguments because the marriage is over—and that was for the best," she told him, squeezing his shoulder as she walked past him. "That's all. Truce?"

Ned reached up to wrap his hand around her wrist.

Zaria looked down at his hand and then into his face.

He turned his head quickly and pressed a kiss to the backside of her hand.

Zaria rolled her eyes heavenward.

"I ain't gonna lie—you sure been looking damn good lately."

Zaria arched a brow as she saw the desire in his eyes as he watched her like a dog salivating over a meaty bone.

"Since we called this truce and all, why don't we celebrate it with a little fun . . . for old time's sake?" he said, reaching up to palm her buttocks.

Zaria's mouth fell wide open before she composed herself and realized this was a moment a lot of first wives longed for. "Stand up," she said huskily with a wink as she licked her lips.

Ned jumped to his feet. "That's what I'm talking 'bout," he said eagerly, almost panting. "I'm gone *tear* that thing up."

"You used to like it nice and wet, too, huh?" she asked him.

"Woman, what you talking about?"

"Like water in a deep well, huh?" Zaria asked huskily.

Ned shivered and nodded.

Zaria took his chair and turned it around to face her. "Sit," she told him, placing her hands on his chest to gently push him.

"Right here in the restaurant?" he asked in amazement, looking around.

"Just sit."

As soon as he did, Zaria removed her coat and

stepped back to pose like she was on the cover of *Essence.* "My grandma told me that one thing about a man is he never misses all that water till his well run dry," Zaria said.

Ned looked hesitant.

"So I want you to sit right there and watch *all of this* as I walk away, because you will never ever—never ever—*ever* touch, taste, sniff, or see this good juice between my thighs again. Ever. When it comes to you, boo-boo, the well is bone dry. O-kay?"

With a little laugh that was slightly mocking, Zaria did a dramatic turn and sashayed away from him with an exaggerated movement of her hips. "Oh, and you tell the second Mrs. Ali that the first one says what's up," she flung over her shoulder.

"Come on, Zaria, stop playing," he called behind her.

Zaria just laughed and kept it moving on out the door.

She couldn't wait until next week to tell Dr. Dennison all about it.

Kaleb pulled the Mule to a stop near the front of his property. He stood up on the vehicle and shaded his eyes from the sun as he looked at the land where he planned to place his dairy store. The land had already been cleared and leveled. On Monday, the county was coming out to put in an oversized driveway to connect the land to the front highway, keeping what he hoped to be a good bit of traffic from having to go through his actual farm or the portion of his property where his house sat.

He glanced down at his watch just as a large black Ford F-150 with JAMISON CONTRACTORS on the side came over the hill and down to park where he sat. Kaleb hopped down off the Mule as the Jamison twins climbed out of the truck and walked over to him.

Seeing the identical twins made him think of Zaria's daughters, which led to thoughts of Zaria. His heart tugged at a vision of her swamped by his clothing, her face free of all that makeup and her hair up in a ponytail as he showed her his farm. She never looked more beautiful to him.

"What's up, fellas?" Kaleb said, reaching out to shake Deshawn's and Devon's hands.

The twins were just nearing their forties and had already established their construction company as one of the best in the southeast. They were known for their hard work, their dedication to finishing a job on budget and on time, and their honesty. They had done the renovations on Kaleb's home years ago, and he couldn't think of anyone else he would trust with this newest extension of his business.

"Who did the excavation?" Devon asked. He was the more serious of the two brothers. "They did one helluva job."

Kaleb nodded. "I did mostly. My family chipped in a couple of years ago and bought some farming equipment and some excavation equipment."

"Shit, if farming slows up, you could go into land clearing, Kaleb," Deshawn said.

Kaleb shook his head. "I'm barely getting enough sleep now. I got enough on my plate."

"Better too much work than not enough," Devon said.

Kaleb eyed them. "How's everything going with y'all?"

"We're still going pretty strong, considering. It's just so many of our subcontractors are going out of business that we're having a hard time finding people of the quality and caliber we want to work with."

"And that's important," Kaleb said, understanding completely.

"That's *damn* important," Deshawn said.

Kaleb spent the next hour going over his plans for the dairy store with the brothers. They walked the land and took notes based on Kaleb's specifications. And if they offered a better alternative in terms of cost or timing, Kaleb was open to their suggestions. He trusted them.

"The last thing I ask for, fellas, is some of Chloe's cooking at my grand opening just like when my house was done. Deal?" Kaleb asked, looking at both men.

Devon's wife, Chloe, was an ex-supermodel who retired young from the business and moved back to her mother's hometown in Holtsville to build a home and capture Devon's heart. The woman cooked like she was eighty years old—that good old-fashioned soul food.

Devon patted his stomach. "Good food and good loving can't be beat."

As the men laughed and made their way back

to the vehicles, Kaleb thought of Zaria again. He remained behind after the men took their leave.

If I could be the woman you wanted—the woman you need—I would.

Kaleb shook his head to free it of her image and her words. No need to look back. He was determined to stay focused on his business and the business of getting over her so that he could be open to bringing someone else into his life permanently. Pining away for her and thinking of the coulda, woulda, and shouldas was pointless.

Kaleb got back onto his Mule and zoomed over the land and across his farm to his house. He parked the Mule and climbed into his pickup to head over to his parents'. He was starving and too tired to cook. It was nice to be able to run home to his parents' for a home-cooked meal, but he was anxious for the days he could walk into his own home and smell the dinner his wife was cooking just for him.

The sun faded and the night chill immediately filled the air. When he reached his parents', he was reluctant to leave the heat of his truck. Knuckling up, he left the truck and dashed up the stairs and into the house. The fireplace was ablaze and the smell of food was in the air.

He heard tiny feet against the hardwood floors, and soon his nephew KJ came barreling at him. "Uncle Kaleb. What's up, man?"

Kaleb laughed as he scooped him up and tossed KJ's chubby frame high into the air and then caught him with ease, causing the toddler to burst into a fit of giggles. "Again, Uncle Kaleb.

Again," KJ pleaded, sounding breathless with excitement.

"This is the *last* time," he said, just like he said a dozen times before and each time the little toddler smiled him into yet another toss.

"Okay," KJ said, clapping his pudgy hands.

Shaking his head, Kaleb tossed the toddler up again and caught him.

"Uh-oh," KJ said.

"Oh shit," Kaleb said, a millisecond before his nephew puked all over the side of his face and down the front of his shirt.

KJ looked wide-eyed. "Aw, man," he said as his uncle set him down on the ground. "Sowry, Uncle Kaleb."

Kaleb kept his right eye shut and looked down at KJ with his left. "No biggie. It happens," he said, reaching down to rub his nephew's head before he made his way to his parents' guest bathroom to clean up.

When Kaleb turned to leave, he nearly tripped over KJ, who was standing in the doorway watching him. Kaleb grabbed a clean washcloth and wet it to clean around his nephew's mouth. "See, all clean. We straight?"

KJ nodded, "We straight," he mimicked.

He grabbed his nephew's chubby hand and they walked into the den. His father was sitting in his recliner watching the evening news. KJ went running up to climb into his grandpa's ever-available lap.

"Hey, Kaleb," Kael said, tickling his grandson.

"Where's everybody?" Kaleb asked.

"Your mama's in the kitchen on that phone and cooking. The rest of the crew are all home," he said. "Kahron came over with this little one here before he headed home, and my grandboy wanted to stay with Grandpa. Ain't that right, man?"

Kael held his large hand out and KJ slapped his little hand against the palm. "Stay with Grandpa," he said.

"I'm just gonna grab me a plate and head home," Kaleb said. "Or I might go to Charlie's and play a little poker."

"A'ight," Kael said, his attention already turned back to the news.

Kaleb headed out of the room.

"Hey, your brother and Jade called. They're going to the justice of the peace next month, and your mother and I are having a big reception here for them."

"It's about time," Kaleb said with a big grin.

"He wasn't sure about asking you to be his best man," Kael said.

Kaleb frowned deeply. "I'm straight, Pops," he said. "I'll call him."

"I figured the same. That's why I told you."

Kaleb squeezed his dad's shoulder and patted it before he reached for his cell phone from his pocket. He called their landline number first. It rang just twice.

"Big Kaleb in the house," Jade said.

"You two finally jumping the broom, huh?"

Kaleb asked with a genuine grin, his eyes crinkling at the corners. "It's about time."

"Yeah, nothing big and without all the la-de-da," she said.

"It's about the marriage and not the wedding, right?" he said.

"Right."

"Where my baby bubba?" he asked, turning to look out the window of the den as he crossed one arm over his massive chest.

"Right here . . . but I wanted to talk to you first," Jade said.

"Listen, I'm a big boy. I can handle seeing my brother get married to the woman he loves without jumping off a roof," he drawled.

"That's Kaeden's opinion on how you feel," Jade said. "I wanted to apologize in advance for anything my mama might do at the reception."

Kaleb made a face. "Your mama?" he asked.

Jade sighed. "Yes, she heard that you're available and has made it quite clear—no matter how much I begged her not to—that she is going to be just the cougar you need."

Kaleb felt his neck warm as he hung his head and laughed. "Now, no more older women for me," he said good-naturedly.

"Baby, I know my mama, and I'm just putting out a pre-apology and warning you to have your guard up."

"I will," Kaleb assured her.

"Okay, here's Kaeden."

He listened as she handed off the phone.

"So I'm the best man," Kaleb said.

"I want you to be," Kaeden said. "You a'ight with that?"

"I'm good. I just need a time and a place and what color suit to pull from my boudoir," he said jokingly.

"I just never saw you take this long to get over a girl before."

Kaleb shrugged. "I never really been in love before, and I just want to get Zaria out of my system and clear out all our baggage so I can start new and fresh with someone else. I'm just chilling out, but you know me—I could be running through girls right now, it's just not the right move, you know. I'm focused on some other things."

"So we're good?" Kaeden asked.

"I don't know about you, but I'm happy as hell for my little brother," he said honestly.

"A'ight," Kaeden said, sounding like their father.

"Let me see what Mama got cooking in this kitchen."

Kaleb closed the phone and slipped it back into his pocket.

"Hey."

He turned to look over at his father. "Don't be around here with blue balls waiting to fall out of love. There's plenty of women looking for a booty call just like you, boy," his father warned.

Kaleb flung his head back and laughed. "Man. Pops, you tripping."

"Humph, Pops ain't tripping. Pops still dipping," he said. "Ask your mama if you don't believe it."

Kaleb frowned. "Man, I don't need to think of you with *my mama,* and I'm about to eat, man."

"Matter of fact, as soon as you bounce and we rock this one to sleep, Pops gots some work to do," Kael assured him, loving to tease his sons.

"Let me get my plate and get out of y'all way, then," Kaleb said over his shoulder.

"Got work to do," KJ mimicked.

Kael chuckled long after Kaleb waved his hand at them and walked into the kitchen.

CHAPTER 12

Two weeks later

Zaria was in line at Home Depot when she felt the hair on the back of her neck stand on end. She shifted the scarf she wore around her neck, thinking it was irritating her skin. When her neck tingled again as she stepped forward in line, she snatched the scarf off and pushed it down into her oversized tote in irritation. When she felt a nervous energy shimmer over her body, she froze and frowned before waving her hand dismissively. *That would be insane,* she thought at the idea of even being in the vicinity of Kaleb would set off her triggers.

As she moved forward to the register, she smiled at the cashier as she lifted the boxes of new light fixtures from the cart onto the counter to be rung up.

"Kaeden, don't touch that. You know you allergic to everything," a deep, masculine voice said.

Kaleb had an allergy-prone brother named

Kaeden, Zaria thought before turning to look down the length of the line of customers. Her heart slammed against her chest to see Kaleb and his three brothers at the end of the line. And what a sight the four of them made with the tall and broad physiques, good looks, and silvery hair.

She jerked back around, feeling breathless as she closed her eyes and covered her mouth with a quivering hand.

"Ma'am, are you okay?" the cashier asked.

Zaria nodded and gave him a big smile that was as fake as a six-dollar pack of weave hair. "Um, I'm not going to get these after all. I'm so sorry," she leaned in to whisper to him. "I'm sorry."

She ducked her head and walked out the doors of the home-repair chain as quickly as she could, not stopping until she was surrounded by the early November winds. She rushed on her heels to her VW Bug, but she froze with her key in hand before she turned and looked back at the store. The man she loved—still loved—was in there.

She thought about the last time she saw him—at Oscar's with another woman—and she turned to open her car door.

Zaria, you have spent too much time focused on the negatives of your relationship with Ned that you are denying the many positives that were in your relationship with Kaleb.

Dr. Dennison. Zaria faithfully went to her weekly sessions and felt like it was worth the money. But these days, little bits of her wisdom or insight came to her like she had a mini Dr. Dennison sitting on her shoulder like the Great Gazoo from the cartoon *The Flintstones.*

Zaria turned again and looked at the store. Was running into him a sign? What were the odds that a woman who never frequented a hardware store would run into the man she pined for on the one and only time she planned to visit one?

What if Kaleb Strong is the one for you? Your soul mate? What are you missing out on because of your fear?

Zaria pushed her car door shut with her butt before she headed back toward the store. If nothing else, she wanted to lay eyes on Kaleb again. Just once.

The four brothers were walking out just as she was about to step through the automatic doors. "Hello, gentlemen," Zaria said, smiling at the brothers before she turned to look up at Kaleb. Her heart was racing and she felt a swell of love for him fill her. "Hello, Kaleb."

He squinted his eyes as he looked down at her and shoved his hands into the pockets of his charcoal wool peacoat. "Zaria," he said in greeting.

"Nice seeing you, Zaria," Kade said.

"Yes, it's nice seeing y'all too," she said, her chest light and her heart fluttering like butterfly wings as she struggled not to release emotional tears. Just being in Kaleb's presence made her feel more alive than she had in weeks. She wanted nothing more—nothing more in the world—than to wrap her arms around him and feel hin

Just feel his body against hers.

"Hey, my girl and I are getting married
couple of weeks," Kaeden said, reaching in
pocket for a small square invitation. "You

come to the reception. We just bought some things for it."

Zaria looked at Kaleb, his expression stoic, before she reached out and took the invitation. "I just might come," she said with a smile.

The brothers all nodded before they walked away, leaving her and Kaleb standing there alone. He didn't walk away from her, but he looked off into the distance at something—at anything but her.

"You look good, Kaleb," she said, reaching out to lightly tug his coat jacket.

"I didn't fall apart when you dumped me, if that's what you mean," he said.

Zaria felt a pang in her chest. "You're too strong a man for that, Kaleb, and I know that," she told him softly.

Kaleb finally rested those deep-set eyes on her. "You don't have to feel obligated to come to the reception," he said.

"If you don't want me to come, I won't, Kaleb," she said.

He shrugged before he looked away again. "It's up to you. It's not my party."

"I'm sorry, Kaleb."

He looked back down at her. "For what?" he ...is tone clipped.

...es filled with tears. "For hurting you."

...ked away with another shrug of ... good."

...ought was right."

...u got to choose all by yourself

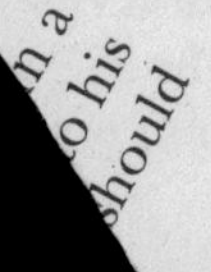

what was right for us?" he asked, his voice hard and his eyes angry when they landed on her.

Tell him. Tell him you love him.

But she couldn't. She couldn't.

"It was good seeing you, Kaleb," she said, reaching out again to tug on the edge of his coat.

"A'ight," he said before brushing past her to walk away.

Zaria clutched at her throat, her emotions nearly strangling her as her head hung low to her chest. It took all of her will not to crumble to the ground.

That energy between them radiated over her body. She knew before he spoke that he had come back to stand behind her. She couldn't turn. She didn't want him to see her tears.

"I never called that girl or even wanted to call her until you and I were over."

Zaria bit her bottom lip, loving him even more for that. He was a man of honor, and he wanted her to know that he never dishonored her. When Zaria finally turned, he was gone. Her eyes searched the parking lot just in time to see him climb into the back of a four-door pickup.

She watched the vehicle until it left the parking lot.

Kaleb was silent on the ride back from North Charleston to Holtsville. Thankfully, his brothers let him be. They were men in love, and they understood that their brother was in the middle of an emotional storm, and it was particularly important because of all the brothers, Kaleb was the one who kept his emotions close to his chest.

When they walked out of the store and he laid eyes on Zaria standing there, like she walked out of his thoughts, he almost had to shake his head to make sure it was really her. And then the wind brought him her familiar scent and she was smiling up at him, unsure of his reaction.

And that familiar vibe that hadn't faded one bit was still there. Still between them. Still undeniable. He had felt as if a jolt of electricity was sent through his body, and he had to shove his hands into his pockets to keep from touching her, grabbing her, pressing his hands to her face and kissing her. It took all of his might to resist.

To keep looking away from her at the trees, at people pushing their carts, at random cars driving by, to keep from looking into her eyes and seeing her beauty. Every second made him love her even more.

He had taken small steps to get over her, but that one chance meeting would be a setback. The words *I love* had rested on the tip of his tongue from the moment he saw the tears well up in her eyes. He literally had to swallow them back, because only he knew how vulnerable and exposed he was when he said the words the last time and she told him good-bye in response.

Kaleb had to be free. He had to put distance between them. To begin his recovery. To not be affected by what looked like love in her eyes. He'd thought he'd seen that look before. He had been wrong.

When he first climbed back into the truck, he had watched her through the window and had seen her watching them. It was the action of a woman in love, but then why not say it? *Why not just say it?* he wondered.

Because she doesn't love me.

She misses my dick.

She even missed the good times we shared.

But she doesn't love me.

Period. Point blank.

That hurt like a motha.

But . . . something with Zaria wasn't adding up. He couldn't figure the woman out for the life of him. If it was just a fling, then why the tears? Why the sad eyes? Why the look of love? What was that all about?

As soon as they got back to their parents' ranch, the brothers saw Kaitlyn sitting on the porch looking decidedly petulant. Kaleb bit back a smile and shook his head as he jogged up the porch. "What's wrong now?" he asked, playfully brushing her cheek with his fist.

"My friends are all going to Paris and Daddy won't let me go," she said, sighing like the world was over.

"Let you go?" Kahron asked. "You're twenty-four."

Kaitlyn crossed and uncrossed her legs. "Okay, *fine.* He won't pay for me to go."

"I'm out of that," Kahron said, backing into the house with the large box he held.

"Me too," Kade said, climbing into his pickup.

"Tell Pops I went to check on the new paddocks real quick."

He pulled off and headed away from the house and toward the farm on the far side of the property.

Kaitlyn eyed Kaleb, who instantly shook his head. "You know I have a lot of money tied up in the dairy store. Sorry. I'm on a spending freeze."

She sighed. "It's just eight grand."

"*Just* eight grand?" Kaleb balked.

Kaeden chuckled. "It must be nice on planet Kaitlyn," he drawled. "*Just* eight grand."

Kaeden disappeared in the house as well with a large box of supplies.

"I am going to Paris," Kaitlyn said, her voice determined.

"Good luck with that, kiddo," Kaleb said, jogging down the stairs to walk over the same well-worn path Kade had driven to reach the farm.

"Where you going?" she called out. "Sunday dinner almost ready."

"I'll be back," he said over his shoulder, reaching into his pocket for his snug sweater cap to pull down on his head.

He was going to ride the property and just wanted to be alone. He knew if he told his sister that she would have joined him. Kaitlyn loved horseback riding just as much as her brothers—well, all except Kaeden.

Kaleb made his way to the barn quickly and saddled one of the horses himself. It was Sunday, and all of the ranch hands were off for the day. Soon he was guiding his horse toward the north of the property where Kade and his father grazed their cattle. He rode at a leisurely trot, not looking to work the animal and not looking for a workout for himself. He just wanted the peace and the quiet. Reflection couldn't be accomplished around noise, and as much as he loved his family, they were loud when they all were gathered in one place.

Growing up, he would sneak away from them and just enjoy the quiet. The sounds of nature. The rustle of trees. The cries of birds above. That brought him peace, and it was some semblance of peace that he searched for now.

When he came to the break in trees, a less knowledgeable eye would think there was nothing to be explored, but Kaleb guided the horse through the break and down a path that ran along a stream and eventually came to a small circle of trees. Dismounting, he led the horse to a safe clearing and loosely tied his reins around a sturdy branch of a tree.

He had discovered this little piece of earth when he was just ten or eleven. There were many occasions he would grab a horse and come here—whether to read or to play his handheld video games or to just lie in the middle of the circle under the heavy blanket of leaves to nap during a sudden rain.

He grabbed the rolled-up blanket tied to the saddle and folded it thickly, then dropped it on the ground in front of a tree and settled back, leaning against the trunk and closing his eyes to listen to the sounds of the water running gently and the fall winds causing the browning leaves to rustle against one another.

He would have loved to bring Zaria here. Although he had never shown his hideaway to anyone, not even his brothers, he could have easily seen him and Zaria there in the circle huddled together naked beneath blankets with nothing but the sounds of nature and their sex cries filling the air.

Kaleb released a heavy breath. He wasn't over her and was beginning to wonder if he ever really would be. What would that mean for the woman he chose to marry one day? She would be running second place to his feelings and his desires and his want of Zaria.

He opened his eyes and looked over to the stream. His breath caught in his throat as a vision of Zaria, nude and wet emerging from beneath the waters, shone before him, playing out like a movie in his head. . . .

Zaria held her hand up to run back over her hair, squeezing the water from the ends. The movement caused her breasts to be thrust forward and moisture clung in droplets from her nipples. She smiled at him as she came to bend to her knees beside him on the blanket where he lay naked and hard and waiting for her. She massaged her soft hands across his hair-covered chest, teasing the tight brown nipples before outlining the jagged grooves of his six-pack and then stroking the tight curls surrounding the base of his hardness. With a wicked smile and a little lick of her lips, she wrapped her fingers around him tightly, causing his hips to thrust up off the ground. She blew a cool stream of air against the tip.

Kaleb shivered as he entwined his fingers in her hair.

She used her tongue to circle the tip before pursing her lips to release another stream of air that made him cry out and arch his back. He tensed his body, trying to prepare for the feel of her mouth in the seconds just before she took his hard heat into her mouth so deeply that the smooth tip touched the back of her throat as she circled the length of him with her tongue.

"Zaria," he cried out roughly, squeezing his eyes shut as grabbed the ground around him so roughly that a patch of dirt filled his hand. He flung it away.

Zaria hummed as she tasted his drizzle and sucked the tip deeply as if to draw life from him. She enjoyed the taste of him against her tongue. The smell of him filling her nostrils. The soft curls of his hairs teasing his chin. "Good?" she asked, her words barely intelligible because her mouth was filled with him.

Kaleb nodded vigorously as he swallowed over a lump in his throat. "More," he begged.

Zaria used her hands to guide his thighs wide open and then moved to sit between them. She wet him before she wrapped both of her hands around him and massaged the length of him from tip to base deeply and slowly as if milking him. She bent so low her back ached, but she didn't care. She massaged the base and took the head into her mouth to tease and taunt and titillate the tip with her tongue with tiny featherlight flickers and licks.

"You know I love you, Kaleb," she sighed, rubbing the length of him against the side of her face and against her mouth before she again tasted him.

"And I love you." He moaned, his entire body shivering as he felt his release building. He gasped hotly as the

tip became supersensitive to her touch and taste. "I'm gonna come."

"No . . . not yet," Zaria said softly, releasing him just long enough to move up and straddle his hips before she reached to hold him as she guided her tight, warm, and wet core down onto him slowly.

She released a dozen tiny cries as she took him into her inch by inch, trying to adjust to the feel of him spreading her walls to accommodate him. "Kaleb," she cried out once all of him was hidden deep within her.

Zaria sat up straight and let her head fall back, thrusting her breasts forward for him to massage and tease her nipples. Biting her bottom lip, she reached behind her to grab his thighs as she began to shift her hips back and forth in a steady and even motion that caused her walls to tighten down on the length of him like a vise.

She rocked her hips. Back and forth. Back and forth. Back and forth.

Kaleb leaned up to watch the lips of her core surrounding his thickness as it appeared and disappeared inside of her with each movement of her hips. He reached behind her to tightly grasp her buttocks and tightened his buttocks to thrust his dick up deeper into her.

"Ah!" Zaria gasped sharply, digging her nails into his flesh as she began to circle her hips, being sure to pop her hips, at the end of each circle.

"Shit!" Kaleb swore, soundly slapping her buttocks to echo in the air.

WHAP!

"Ride that dick," he told her thickly, his hooded eyes looking up at her and enjoying the looks of passion and pleasure on her contorted face.

Zaria picked up the pace of her grinds like she heard a sultry reggae beat in the air around her. She thrust her hips harder, pulling on the length of him. Wanting to draw out his seed with a force that would shake him to his core.

"Come in me," Zaria begged, opening her eyes to look down into his face as her sweat dripped off her body down onto him like a slow drizzle of rain. "Come in me. I want your baby, Kaleb. Give me a baby."

Kaleb's eyes jerked open, and he sat up straight, his heart pounding as hard as the pulse of the vein running alongside his hard erection. He released a heavy breath and covered his face with both of his hands.

He bent his legs and placed his arms atop them as he let his head hang, looking down at his thick hardness straining against his jeans as it ran down the top of his thigh.

What am I going to do with her? he wondered, because he knew that things between them were far from over.

As soon as Zaria walked through the front door, she dropped everything in her hand onto her coffee table and turned to the couch to fall promptly onto it. Zaria shifted to her side on the couch, and her eyes fell on her cell phone sitting there. Mocking her. Nagging her. Tempting her. *Call him. Call him, Zaria.*

She closed her eyes, feeling fatigued and completely drained of energy and will. Seeing Kaleb had shaken her to the core, and she still hadn't recovered. How could she when he was all she thought about during her ride home?

She loved him. Completely.

She missed him. Totally.

She wanted him. Unabashedly.

Zaria shifted over onto her back and covered her eyes with her forearm. She thought of the countless nights they had shared right here in her house. Laughing. Playing. Talking. Making love.

She smiled at a vision of her and Kaleb making love in front of her fireplace in the dead of summer. They both had wanted to enjoy the experience, so they turned the air as high as it would go—and still sweated like crazy. The moisture had caused their bodies to easily slide and glide over one another, intensifying their play. . . .

As the sound of the lit log crackled inside the fireplace, Zaria dug her knees into the plush padding of the area rug as the fire cast a bronzed glow on their naked bodies as she rode him. She leaned down to taste Kaleb's mouth before sitting up straight again and continuing to work her hips in a slow circle that pleased them both. Kaleb brought his hands up to tease her nipples as her sweat ran down her body like droplets of rain on a windowpane.

She picked up the pace, working her hips in a grind that rivaled the baddest reggae dancer. She bit her bottom lip as she rode him hard and fast—her heart pounding in her ears with the vibrancy of a steel drum. Her body tingled as that crazy energy they created swirled around them with the force of a storm with the power to amaze and destroy. "Kaleb," she gasped, leaning forward to clutch at his hard chest as she worked nothing but her hips, sending her wet and tight core up and down the length of him as she also worked him rhythmically with the muscles of her walls.

"Get that nut, baby," he moaned up to her, his face fierce and warriorlike as he watched her like a hawk by the firelight.

"Come in me," Zaria begged, biting her lips with a moan as she bent down to grasp his face and kiss him deeply. Their eyes locked. "Come in me. I want your baby, Kaleb. Give me a baby."

Kaleb's eyes sharpened on her as an energy like nothing he knew filled him as he grabbed her hips, bent his legs to press his feet into the plush carpeting, and then began to thrust upward into her against her walls. He was relentless. Each thrust more powerful than the last but never hurting her. Just fulfilling her. Completing her. With power and passion.

Zaria spread her knees atop him, opening herself to him. "I want your baby," she whispered again into his mouth with a soft smile.

"I want you to come with me," he said, his voice shaky as he felt his release building.

Zaria began to move her hips, meeting him thrust for thrust. "I am," she told him, before she released a deep guttural moan and clutched wildly at the carpet as explosions went off inside her.

Kaleb cried out as he felt each and every spasm that sent his seed deep within. . . .

Zaria's eyes popped open and she scrunched up her face in confusion.

What started out as a nice and steamy trip down memory lane had changed into something she didn't recognize. *Me? Begging Kaleb to fill me up with a baby?*

She sat up on the couch and frowned. Deeply.

That definitely never happened.

Her babies were over twenty, and her baby-making days were *so* over.

Zaria laughed and waved her hand dismissively as she lay back on the couch. She couldn't wait to see what Dr. Dennison had to say about that—especially since Zaria has expressed in length that she was too old to be making babies and she couldn't care less if J.Lo and Ms. Halle Berry had done it. It was not on her to-do list. Nada.

"No," Zaria said out loud, putting it out into the universe, sitting up again. "No. No. Nooooo."

She laughed. "My babies are old enough to have babies of their own. Puhleeze," she said, lying down again.

And Zaria knew Kaleb wanted beautiful, brown babies to bounce. She knew that and she wasn't doing it, so why tie his life up? "And why have that stupid vision, dream, nightmare, whatever," she said aloud.

Zaria sat up again and reached for her pocketbook. "'Cause that's impossible," she said again, pulling out her old-school daily planner. She opened it to November. Then she flipped to October.

She was looking for the tiny red X on the days she had her cycle. Closing the book and chuckling again, she clapped her hands and did a little dance in her seat. "Okay. Alrighty, then," she said, licking her lips as she opened the book. Again.

And checked November. Again.

And then October. Again.

She flung that away from her as if it were a mouse. She sat back on the couch with an eyebrow arched as she thought hard, trying to remember the annoyance of going through a cycle last month.

But there was nothing to remember. She did not have a cycle last month and none so far this month.

The baby talk made her think of her cycle, but then she didn't remember having a dang on cycle and thought the daily planner would help—but it didn't. Zaria began to breathe deeply, almost hyperventilating, as she felt a muscle or a vein, a spasm or *something*, tic over her left eye.

Her eyes shifted left and right and back again. "Condoms. We used condoms. I'm the condom *queen*. He's the condom *kiiing*. We're condom royalty. We can make condom commercials. We made beautiful condom-filled love. Nice and secure condoms."

Except . . .

The sound of Zaria swallowing over a lump in her throat echoed.

Except their last time by her front door when they got caught up in the heat of that argument.

Zaria bit the side of her thumbnail as her eyes shot over to the wall where they did the deed. The condomless deed.

"No. No. My old ass is just going through menopause or some shit," Zaria screamed, jumping to her feet. "I'm celebrating, 'cause no more pads. No more cycles. No more PMS. No more Motrin. No more granny panties. Right? Right?"

She fell back down onto the sofa and dropped her head into her hands.

CHAPTER 13

After a hard day's work, Kaleb drove his Mule over to the site for the dairy store. The Jamisons had already framed up the structure and assured him the roof would be going on that Monday. They were done for the day, but he left his vehicle and walked over to the structure, tilting his head back to take it all in.

If felt good for his plans to come together. A lot of the townspeople let him know they were ready to frequent the store for the fresh dairy products. And Kaleb hadn't done one bit of advertising yet. In a small town like Holtsville, much wasn't needed. News of any and everything new spread fast around these parts. And people didn't mind asking questions.

Kaleb gave the structure one last walk-through and then glanced at his watch. He had to get going. His parents were giving Jade and Kaeden a pre-wedding dinner just for the family. He still needed to get washed and changed.

An old truck went by on the road, and Kaleb

threw his hand up in greeting. The driver, Lee Yates, blew his horn twice briefly. Everyone knew Lee's truck. It was as small as a Matchbox car but as loud as a tractor trailer.

He drove the Mule across the flatlands, feeling the cold air biting against his cheeks as the skies turned streaks of orange, lavender, and dark blue as the sun descended. It was a chilly but beautiful evening.

I wonder what Zaria's doing?

In the week since he'd seen her, she had filled his thoughts during the day and plagued his dreams at night. Many times he would start to call her and then force himself to close his phone.

Kaleb would admit only to himself that he feared being rejected and put off by her again. Why would he open himself up to that?

He undressed as he rushed inside his house and across the living area to his bedroom. He paused at the door and turned, flipping the switch to bask the entire house with light.

Kaleb's eyes flittered over the entire house. It felt empty and cold to him. It felt lonesome. It felt like a shell of what it could be. There was no laughter. There was no Zaria.

He had been on this great search for the love of his life and he had stumbled upon Zaria. At first he saw her as an obstacle or a rest stop before he moved on to better things. But his heart had taken over from his mind and he had fallen for her. Hard.

The more he wrestled with everything that happened between them, everything that had been said and done, the more confused he became about Zaria's feelings.

She never said she loved him. But she never said she didn't.

He believed in fate. He believed in destiny.

As time went on and his love didn't fade—even in the face of his anger toward her—he believed that Zaria Ali was the one God meant just for him. Something in him knew she loved him. He knew it.

They could get past the age difference, her issues with her divorce . . . even whether they would have kids, but he didn't think he could have a full life without her laughter, her touch, her sex, and her all with him, by his side, having his back while he had hers.

Giving his house one last look, he rushed into the bathroom for a shower. Afterward, he quickly changed into a cable-knit sweater and jeans, but instead of heading in the direction of his parents' ranch, he sped toward Summerville. As soon as he turned into Zaria's yard and parked next to her little VW Bug, he raced up the stairs and knocked on the door.

He had to believe that she loved him just as much as he loved her.

And if he fell on his face, if he got turned away, at least he would know that he fought one last time for his heart.

The door opened but one of the twins stood there.

He looked past her inside the house but the couch was empty. "Hey . . ."

"Meena," she supplied as she leaned against the door and looked up at him.

"Meena. Right. Is your mom home?" he asked, easing his hand into the front pocket of his jeans.

She scrunched up her face. "I thought you two broke up?"

Kaleb swallowed back his irritation. Another of their obstacles on the road to happily-ever-after were her twins. Telling her to mind her own damn business wasn't a step in the right direction.

"We did," he said, nodding. "So is she here?"

"I thought you lived in Holtsville?" she asked.

Kaleb did a five count and flexed his shoulders. "Yes, yes, I do."

She shook her head pitifully. "That's a long ride without calling first," she said.

"Because she's not home?" he offered, with just one last smidgen of his patience.

"You really should have, like, flowers and candy, you know," she said. "I'm just saying."

Kaleb hung his head briefly and chuckled to relieve his irritation. "Yes, your mother loves lilies and I should have sent her some."

"And the candy?" she added, chastising him.

"Your mother doesn't like sweets," he said.

Meena nodded and applauded. "Good answer."

Kaleb looked down at her and saw the twinkle in her eyes. "You're enjoying this, aren't you."

"Pretty much," she agreed.

"And are we playing twenty questions for me to win an answer to my question?" he asked.

"Oh, you got jokes," she said.

No, what I have is a switch, he thought.

The cell phone in her hand rang and she

looked down at it. "Ooh, got to take this call," she said, stepping back to close the door.

Kaleb casually stuck his foot out.

She frowned as she looked down at it and then up at him. "Yes?" she said, sounding annoyed.

"Your mother?"

"She and my sister went somewhere," Meena said with a shrug.

"You'll let her know I stopped by, okay? A'ight. See you later . . . Meena." Kaleb turned and crossed the porch.

"Yup."

He was barely down the stairs before the door closed firmly. In his pickup truck, he pulled his cell phone from the middle console and dialed Zaria's cell phone. It went straight to voice mail. He didn't bother to leave a message. What he had to say was best said face-to-face.

Zaria sat up on the couch and eyed her daughter. "Is he gone?" she asked, holding her powered down cell phone in her hand.

"Yes, ma'am," Meena said, coming over to stand behind the couch and look down at her mom. "You really should talk to your baby daddy."

Zaria cut her eyes at her daughter. "I don't know if I'm pregnant," she said.

"Um, Neema and I found like ten pregnancy kits in the trash when we got here this morning," Meena said. "Sorry to tell you, but you're pregnant."

"I need confirmation with blood work," Zaria said, releasing yet another heavy sigh—possibly her millionth over the last week. "I just wish I could have gotten an appointment sooner."

The front door opened and Neema walked in carrying a bag from Walmart. Zaria frowned. "Neema, I only asked for a heating pad for my back. What is all that you have there?"

"I strolled over to the baby section . . ."

Zaria sighed.

Meena jumped up and down excitedly. "Ooooh, what did you get?"

Neema whipped out a teddy bear.

Meena frowned. "Bo-ring."

Neema arched a brow and looked dead at her twin as she pushed its round belly. Soon the replicated sounds of a mother's womb filled the air.

Meena gave her a thumbs-up. "Awesome."

Neema dug into the bag and pulled out another bear. "In case she's having twins!"

"Double awesome!"

The idea of *that* made Zaria want to faint. "Can I have the heating pad?" Zaria asked, her voice barely heard among the rustling of plastic bags.

"Look what else I have," Neema said, pulling out a bib that read SURPRISE!!!

Zaria eyed them both with a mama stare that used to work. "That is not funny," she said, standing up to grab the bag and dig out the box with the heating pad. She stepped over Meena and Neema huddled on the floor going through the packages like it was Christmas.

Hell, like it was good news.

Zaria headed for her bedroom and tore open the box to lay the pad on the bed before she plugged it in and then lay flat on it.

She had barely got comfortable before they burst into the room. Neema unplugged the cord and Meena unceremoniously rolled her off of the pad to snatch it from under her. "Heating pads are only safe on your arms and legs. It could harm the baby's development," she explained, holding up her iPad.

"You looked that up just that quick?" Zaria asked.

"Technology, Mom. Technology."

Zaria sat up in bed and leaned against the headboard. "Why are you two acting like you know I'm pregnant and like you know I'm having it?" she asked.

They frowned, looked at each other, and frowned deeper, before turning to look at her. "What do you mean?" they asked in unison.

"Girls, I am forty-two years old," she stressed. "This is not wonderful news for me. I raised my babies, and now here you both are working my nerves about something that either isn't or won't be."

"But Halle Berry—"

Zaria closed her eyes and held up both her hands. "I don't want to hear another word about another over-forty celebrity who had a baby," she said, her voice tight.

"Sorry," Neema said.

The sound of her lisp erased the anger from Zaria. "No, it's okay. Y'all just trying to make me feel better and I love y'all for it. Okay?"

They nodded, their mood now decidedly somber.

Zaria tilted her head back against the wall as they quietly left her alone.

She hated that one of their surprise visits home had allowed them to catch the pregnancy kits in the trash before she could get rid of them. She'd much rather go through all of the emotions alone.

Zaria shifted down to lie on the bed on her side.

Kaleb.

She smiled sadly when she thought of him.

All of her initial excitement about him coming to see her disappeared when she thought she might be carrying his child. The child that he wanted so badly. The child that wasn't part of her life plan.

She couldn't tell him the truth. Not yet.

She'd had a week to sit on it and come to grips with it and she still hadn't. All Zaria could hope for was some hormonal imbalance that gave her all of those positives on the pregnancy tests.

Lying flat on her stomach, she slipped her hands under the bulky sweatshirt she wore to press against her flattened abdomen. Okay. Truth.

Zaria knew it. She knew that Kaleb's child was in her womb. Her achy joints weren't from arthritis. Her missing cycles weren't stress. Her tender breasts weren't irritation by the lace of her bras.

She was pregnant.

"You sure snuck up on me," she said softly.

Zaria pulled her shirt back down and rolled over onto her side again. She reached out to dim the lights and clutched her pillows. She felt the picture she kept inside the case and pulled it out to look down at Kaleb's handsome and smiling face.

In a perfect world, she thought, closing her eyes as tears raced down her face.

Kaleb took a sip of his vodka and cranberry juice, smiling into his glass as he watched Kaeden and Jade on the makeshift dance floor in the center of his parents' sizeable two-car garage. Kaeden was giving her the infamous Strong man two-step and Jade danced around him like a firefly.

He was trying his best to have a good time, but his thoughts were filled with Zaria. Now that he was determined to give it one last shot, he was anxious to talk to her. He grabbed his cell phone and tried her cell phone. It still went straight to voice mail again.

"All right, everyone, come on in. Dinner's ready," Lisha Strong said from the doorway leading into the kitchen from the garage.

Kaleb was one of the last to make his way inside the house. He frowned when he saw Deena, Jade's mother, hanging back as well. Sure enough, as soon as she reached the doorway, she appeared at his arm.

"Hi, Kaleb," she said, reaching out to squeeze his hand and stroke his palm with her thumb.

Like Jade, Deena was a beautiful woman. Like Zaria, she definitely didn't look to be in her forties. If she wasn't his brother's mother-in-law, he probably would have made a go for her. But now, as far as he was concerned, she was family and thus off-limits.

"You Strong men sure are fine," she said, linking her arm through his.

"And now, as of tonight, we're all taken," he said, leading her to a chair beside Jade.

Deena frowned. "I thought . . ."

Kaleb shrugged. "We're back together," he said.

Deena looked around. "Is she here? I would love to meet her."

Jade grabbed her mother's arm lightly. "Mama, isn't this nice of the Strongs to throw this dinner?" she asked, motioning for Kaleb to get away.

Kaleb jumped on that hint right away and sat at the other end of the table between Kade and Kahron, who sat across from their wives. His niece Kadina smiled across the table at him. He winked at her as he placed his linen napkin in his lap.

Kael Strong rose to his feet and lightly tapped his fork against his crystal goblet. "On behalf of my lovely wife and myself, I want to thank everyone for joining us to celebrate the wedding of our son Kaeden to beautiful Jade."

Everyone around the table applauded, and Jade's grandfather clapped the loudest from his seat across from his granddaughter. That caused another round of laughter.

Kael cleared his throat. "Family is very important to us Strongs and we extend our love and loyalty to those we consider more than just in-laws," he said warmly, looking down the table at each of his daughters-in-law. "The same way I view Bianca and Garcelle to be just as much my daughters as Kaitlyn is how I view you. Tomorrow just makes it all *official*."

Jade absolutely beamed as she looked up at her future father-in-law with adoration in her eyes. Kaeden leaned over and pressed a kiss to her cheek.

"Please know that you can count on us the same way I make sure that all my kids can count on us for whatever they need. To our new daughter . . . Jade."

Everyone lifted their glasses. "To Jade," they said in unison.

"Jade," KJ called out, holding up his juice box from his booster seat next to Lisha.

The table erupted with laughter and everyone looked down at Kahron and Bianca. They just shook their heads at their son.

Lisha Strong stood. "I won't be as long as my husband, but I did want to say that, um, I really like Jade. You're good for my Kaeden, and once we all got over sending our men alone on a camping trip with such a pretty wilderness guide, I knew that you loved him. He was the one who hung closest to me, and I won't lie and say he's not the one I worried about the most. But now I can rest easy because I know that I have somebody looking out for him just the way I would want. Welcome to the Strong family, Jade." She reclaimed her seat and reached over to pat Kaeden's face and squeeze Jade's hand.

As the toasts continued with Jade's mother in her bright pink wrap dress and gold heels, Kaleb laughed as he saw Jade gather the hem of her mother's skirt in her hand. He guessed she was ready to deliver a little tug if Deena went to the left with her speech.

Thankfully she behaved.

"Just want to thank you all for welcoming my daughter—and me—into your family. I am very happy to have Kaeden as my son-in-law. It's a good feeling for a mother to know that her one and only child has found the love of her life. Nothing in this world could make me happier . . . well, besides some grandbabies," she finished before she reclaimed her seat and received a kiss and hug from Jade.

"Speaking of which . . . I dreamed about fish last night," Lisha Strong said.

"Uh-oh," Jade's grandfather said, smoothing his hands over his slicked-back ponytail.

"Uh-oh is right," Lisha said with an impish grin as she leaned in to look down the table at her children.

"Not us," Bianca assured her, her tight ringlets bouncing as she shook her head. "KJ is more than enough."

Kahron chuckled.

Lisha shifted her eyes to Garcelle and Kade. "No, no, Mamasita," Garcelle said. "Not this time."

The matriarch nodded. "It was you two the last time, wasn't it?"

She lit her eyes on Kaleb. His head was down as he checked the volume of the ringer on his phone. When he looked up, all twelve pairs of eyes were on him. He sat back. "No, not me. Nah, not me. Trust me, I woulda told you way before any fish dreams."

The look she gave Kaitlyn was sharp. "Mama,

puh-leeze. I can barely survive on my allowance alone," she sighed.

Kael gave her a definite side-eye.

Kaeden's and Jade's heads were huddled together, and they also missed all the eyes on them.

"Any reason for the quickie wedding?" Kaitlyn drawled before reaching for her glass of wine.

Deena clapped.

Jade and Kaeden shook their heads. "Maybe next year," Jade said. "I can't rock climb pregnant."

Lisha just gave them a look like "time will tell."

"Okay, if there are no more psychic predictions," Kael said, "let's bless the food and eat."

"No one asked me," Deena said, pretending to look offended.

Jade was the first to laugh and the rest of the table soon joined her.

Kaleb's mind was on Zaria and how badly he wanted her there, knowing that she would perfectly fit into the rambunctious and loud bunch he called family. He knew the night would come when Zaria would be welcomed into the Strong clan. He would accept nothing less.

Zaria awakened late into the night to find both her daughters in bed with her. One behind her and the other at her feet. She smiled, gently climbing from the bed to place blankets over them. The house was cold, and she made her way to the thermostat to adjust the heat.

The lights were still on in the living room, and

she made her way over to the couch where all of the baby items Neema bought were strewn everywhere. Zaria reached down for one of the teddy bears, rubbing its soft fur against the side of her face. She picked up the baby onesies and the bibs, smoothing her hand against their soft cotton texture.

She came around the couch and sat down, picking up the crib mobile. She hit the switch and turned it on and a soft nursery rhyme began to play as the celestial cutouts lit up.

Her life was really about to become about diapers and breast-feeding and middle-of-the-night feedings.

"What have I done?" she asked softly, reaching behind her to massage her lower back.

She rose to her feet just as another spasm radiated across her back. Zaria set the baby things back down on the chair and made her way around it, just wanting to get into her bed—even with two grown women in it with her.

She happened to look down at the couch seat and she gasped at the sight of blood staining the cushion where she sat. Another pain hit her across her back and came around to pierce her belly. She staggered forward and clutched the back of the couch tightly.

"Meena!" she cried out. "Neema!"

Oh my God, I'm losing the baby. Oh my God, I'm losing the baby.

The next time she said the words aloud just as her daughters came running into the living room. "Oh my God, I'm losing my baby," she wailed, tears filling her eyes in an instant as she felt her legs weaken just before she fell to her knees and clutched her stomach desperately.

Kaleb lounged on the sofa in his living room, fully dressed and flipping through the channels on his flat-screen television. He had been home from the prewedding dinner for a couple of hours, and he must have called Zaria's cell phone a dozen times. Her landline number just rang without an answer, and he wouldn't doubt if the twins had the lines tied up or if they were sitting there laughing maniacally as he kept calling the number like a fool.

Turning from some reality show about repo men, he picked up his cell phone again and called her.

"This is Z. You know what to do in five, four, three, two, one. Go."

Beep.

He started to end the call but he pressed the phone back to his face. "Zaria. This is Kaleb. I been trying to call you all night, and I came by your house but your daughter said you weren't there," he began, closing his eyes and leaning his head back against the sofa. "I've been going over this thing between us from start to finish, including the day I saw you at Home Depot, and . . . something doesn't add up for me. Because, see, I love you and I know that this energy, this chemistry, between us is real. To hell with age differences and crap. We got the stuff a lot of people search for their whole lives. I know you love me just as much as I love you, and that means there is nothing in this world we can't get through. Man, to hell with this phone shit. Call me, Zaria. Call me."

Beep.

Kaleb snapped the phone closed and flung it onto the other end of the sofa as he finally kicked off his shoes and twisted his body to lie down.

He didn't know when he finally drifted off to sleep, but the sound of his phone ringing incessantly awakened him and he jumped up, his heart pounding as he looked around for his phone.

Kaleb found it on the floor and flipped it open. "Hello," he said, his already deep voice even more resonant with sleep. "Hello."

"Kaleb . . . this is Meena."

"No more questions, Meena," he said, still half asleep as he rubbed his eyes with the backs of his hands.

"No, it's our mom . . . She's at the hospital in Summerville. Neema and I thought we should call you," she said.

The sound of her voice pushed the last of the sleep from him as he rose to his feet in alarm. "Is she hurt? Is she okay?"

"Just come. We're in the ER, and she's in the back."

Frowning, he nodded even as he stuffed his feet back into his shoes and looked around for his keys. "I'm on my way," he said, patting his pocket and finding his keys before he took long strides to the front door.

Without hesitation, and with fear fueling him on, Kaleb raced from the house and into his pickup to head toward Summerville as fast as his truck allowed.

Chapter 14

You never miss your water till your well run dry. . . .

That saying had never resonated more for Zaria than it did then. For the past week, she had beat herself up for getting pregnant by a younger man while she was a forty-two-year-old divorcée enjoying the second half of her life.

And now she was facing the possibility of a miscarriage.

Zaria closed her eyes and pressed her face deeper into the one ultrasoft pillow they gave her. She shivered, pulling the cover up closer around her ears as the chill of the hospital seemed to seep through her bones. When she closed her eyes, visions of herself swollen and round with child flashed.

She cried as Kaleb filled the vision, stepping up from behind to wrap his arms around her and press his hands to her belly. Or kneeling before her to kiss her belly. Or them lying in bed together with Kaleb spooning from behind as he slept with one hand protectively on her belly.

Image. After image. After image.

And in time the images began to fade, and when she saw herself again, her stomach was flat and Kaleb was walking away from her forever. At forty-two, she had been blessed with a child without one bit of infertility treatment. The Lord had sent a beautiful baby to them. To her and Kaleb.

And Zaria had questioned the blessing. Regretted it. Wished it away.

Now her desire was fulfilled.

She thought back on the debacle at that club and how she had been pressed out the door and fallen to the ground. She thought about the alcohol she had dared to drink as she teetered around on four-inch heels trying to be cute. The heating pad she used to sleep that night.

All things that could have hurt the baby.

What am I going to tell Kaleb? she wondered, imagining his disappointment as she pressed a hand to her belly, wishing she could feel their son or daughter kick her hand in a few months.

Zaria's tears fell harder until her shoulders shook as she gave in to her grief.

The curtain to her room opened and her daughters walked in, both coming to press their warm hands to her legs and her arms as their tears fell too. She was grateful for their presence . . . just as she knew that in time, once the shock wore off, that it would settle in that the baby was indeed a blessing that she would welcome.

"We asked the nurse and she said the doctor would be in to see you next," Neema said, lovingly patting her mother's legs.

Zaria looked up just in time to see the girls share a look. One set of eyes urged the other. Sniffing, Zaria looked back and forth from one to the other. "What's wrong?" she asked.

"We called Kaleb, Ma," Meena said into the quiet as she massaged circles onto Zaria's lower back.

Zaria closed her eyes and nodded as a fresh wave of emotional pain hit her hard. "What did you tell him?" she asked, her voice barely above a whisper as she shifted her eyes to the wall.

"Nothing yet," Meena said.

Zaria grunted a little. "I'll tell him," she said.

Meena and Neema said nothing else as they continued to rub her, trying to bring their mother some measure of comfort as they saw her struggling to cope.

Kaleb barely parked his pickup before he shut it off and ran toward the emergency entrance of the hospital. He nearly slipped and fell in a puddle, but he righted his frame and kept digging until he breezed through the sliding glass door of the hospital. His eyes searched the people in the waiting room before he stepped forward to the glass window of the triage area.

He looked beyond the glass to find it empty. With his heart racing, he knocked on the window. Lightly at first and then with a bit more force that drew the curious stares of the others in the waiting room.

Soon, a young nurse came walking up to the window to slide it open.

"Yes, I was told there's a Zaria Ali admitted here," he said, bending his tall frame over to look directly through the window at her.

"She hasn't been admitted yet. She's waiting to see the doctor," she said.

"What happened?" he asked, his heart still pounding so fast that he was afraid he would pass out and get admitted himself.

"Are you her husband? Or close family?" she asked.

"I was going to propose tonight if that helps," he said, licking the dryness from his mouth.

"I can't release information about a patient—"

"Her daughters, a set of cute twins, called me. Can you let them know that I'm here?" he asked. "My name is Kaleb."

She smiled with a nod and closed the window.

Kaleb stood up to his full six-foot height and crossed his arms over his massive chest, and he stood with his legs wide and his eyes locked on the inner door that he could see through the glass. Every possible scenario of Zaria being hurt played out in his mind, and he felt tortured during every second of the wait.

Soon he spotted the twins, and he watched them through the glass until they disappeared. Seconds later they came through a door and both came walking over to him. Kaleb was taken by surprise when each hugged his neck closely. Surprised and scared shitless.

"Is your mother okay?" he asked, taking in their puffy, red-rimmed eyes.

They both nodded.

"She wants to see you," the one with the ponytail said.

They each took one of his hands and led him to the door, where they released his hands and stepped back. Kaleb gave them one last look and then followed the nurse to the first waiting room. Not knowing what to expect, but anxious to lay eyes on her, he used his arm to pull back the curtain and stepped inside.

Zaria was huddled in a ball on her side, covered by a blanket with nothing but the top of her head showing. For a moment he thought she had passed on. "Zaria . . . Zaria, baby, are you okay?" he asked, stepping up beside her bed to press his hand to her thigh gently. "What happened? What's going on?"

She moved the covers back and her face was puffy and her eyes swollen from crying. "What's wrong? What hurts?" he asked, using his thumbs to wipe away her tears.

That made her cry harder. "Kaleb, I didn't know. I didn't even know," she said, using a crumpled piece of tissue balled in her hand to wipe her nose and eyes.

He bent over and kissed her temple, his face filled with confusion. "Didn't know what?" he whispered near her ear.

"I was pregnant," she said.

Kaleb froze. *Pregnant?*

He instantly thought of his mama's fish dreams. *Me? The fish dream was about me?*

Zaria pressed her hand into his and squeezed

it hard. "I lost the baby," she said to him before she set off with a new round of tears.

Kaleb went through a dozen emotions in the span of a few moments. Surprise. Confusion. Joy. Excitement. Fear. Shock. Sadness. Anger. Confusion again. And lost. Finally, most achingly, he felt the loss.

"Aw, baby," he said as emotions welled up in him.

The child he longed for *and* with the woman he loved and it was over before it even began. How jacked up was that?

"I'm sorry, Kaleb," she said again.

He looked down at her and pressed his lips to her forehead. "It's okay. Are you okay?" Kaleb asked her, feeling numb.

Zaria rolled over onto her back, and she watched as his eyes shifted down to her belly. "Kaleb . . . Kaleb, are you okay?"

He shifted his eyes back up to her, and they were filled with tears as he shook his head. "No," he admitted.

The curtain opened suddenly and the doctor stepped in.

"I'm Dr. Rosen, Mrs. Ali. How are you feeling?" he asked, looking down at her over the rim of his glasses. "Any more pain?"

Zaria shook her head as she struggled to sit up.

"Well, I examined you earlier and we did an ultrasound and looks like everything is fine with little Baby Ali," he said.

Zaria sat up straighter in bed, her hand going to her flat belly while the other was nearly crushed in Kaleb's tight grip.

"Baby Strong," Kaleb said with pride, a huge grin spreading over his face.

The doctor looked confused. "Okay . . . well, looks like Baby Strong is doing fine. Some bleeding during the first trimester of a pregnancy happens. Of course, with your age, Mrs. Ali, I do recommend that you get in to see an ob-gyn as soon as possible to begin your prenatal care."

Zaria dropped her head into her hands. "I feel stupid for overreacting, but I had my last babies over twenty years ago," she said.

The doctor scribbled on her chart. "You did the right thing to come in and get checked. Just take it light for a few days and get your prenatal care going. Okay?"

"I can go home?"

The doctor nodded at Kaleb. "You got this big guy. I'm sure he can handle it."

Kaleb nodded, still smiling like he won one of those mega-state lotteries. "No doubt, Doc. I got it."

Dr. Rosen laughed and gave them a final wave before he walked out.

"We're gonna have a baby," he said, bending down to kiss Zaria on the mouth. "You're gonna have my baby."

Zaria flung the covers back. "I'm ready to get out of this cold place," she said, swinging her feet over the side before rising to her feet.

Kaleb came around to stand before her. He cupped her face with his hands and then dipped his head in to plant tiny kisses on her mouth that caused her to sigh in pleasure. "I love you so much, Zaria," he whispered into her open mouth before he deepened the kiss with a guttural moan.

Zaria brought her hands up to grab the sides of his shirt as Kaleb kissed her with a tenderness and passion that made her feel like she was floating on air. "I love you too," she finally admitted to him as he stepped back to drop to one knee before her.

He kissed her flat belly before he cleared his throat. "This just seems like the right moment to complete what I think was destined to be, Zaria. I believe that although he made you first, God did make you just for me. And I was made for you."

Zaria's mouth fell open in surprise as Kaleb took her hand in his. "I don't want to live this life without you. All this time I been looking for Mrs. Right and you been there the whole time. You've been here the whole time," he said, pointing to his heart. "Marry me, Zaria. Say that you will marry me?" he asked.

"Awwww."

They both turned their heads to find the twins standing there holding each other's hands.

Zaria tapped her foot with nerves and tilted her head back as the emotions again threatened to take her breath. "We don't have to get married because of the baby," she said, looking down into his face and loving him with such intensity. "Because if that's why you're doing this, then I won't say yes. I won't do it."

"The baby?" the twins asked in unison.

Zaria smiled. "I'm still pregnant," she told them.

"Awesome!" they said together before turning to look at each other.

Kaleb cleared his throat, drawing three pairs of

almond-shaped eyes. "Um . . . in the middle of a proposal here?" he said dryly, trying to shift to get comfortable on his knee.

"Sorry," the twins whispered, turning their eyes to their mother and looking on like their own personal soap opera played in front of them.

"Zaria," Kaleb stressed. "Will you marry me?"

"When I'm fifty you'll be—"

"Loving you just as much as I do now, Zaria," he insisted.

The twins sighed dreamily again.

"But how do I know it's not just the baby you want?" she asked, her resolve weakening fast.

"Ma, you are really ruining the moment," Meena drawled.

"Seriously," Neema said with her lisp.

Kaleb could hardly believe the terrible two was cheering him on.

"Seriously," he said, smiling.

Zaria's face softened as she looked down into his eyes and saw his heart. "Yes," she said softly. "Yes. Yes. Yes."

The girls clapped lightly.

Kaleb rose to his feet and looked at her with hot eyes and fierce love as he kissed her with all the passion and promise for more that he had inside of him.

Zaria grunted a little in her sleep as she turned over in bed. It took her a second to register that she wasn't in her own bed and Kaleb's spot was empty. Last night he had insisted that they all come home with him. The girls had been excited about seeing the ranch and the cattle, and even learning to ride a horse. And so they followed behind Kaleb's truck and eventually went to sleep in one of his guest rooms.

She flung back the covers and pulled up the T-shirt Kaleb gave her to sleep in when they went to his house early that morning. She looked down at her flat stomach and pressed her hands against it with a smile.

"Good morning, Baby Strong," she said softly.

Soon her body would swell with the growth of the baby, and Zaria was sure she would look like she swallowed a basketball. Kaleb was just as excited as she'd thought he'd be.

They both had had a lot to deal with in the last twenty-four hours. An emotional reunion in the parking lot. Discovering they were pregnant. Grieving a miscarriage. Discovering there was no miscarriage. Their engagement.

A lot had gone on in a short amount of time.

Zaria spotted her cell phone sitting on the nightstand. She reached for it. She had several voice mail messages.

She dialed her number and entered her code.

"Zaria, this is Hope and Chanci. We haven't heard from you in a minute. Just checking on you, friend. Call us. Love you. Bye."

Are they gonna be surprised.

A baby and a marriage for Zaria Ali? She could hardly believe it herself.

"Zaria. This is Kaleb. I been trying to call you all

night, and I came to your house but your daughter said you weren't there. . . ."

Zaria put the phone on speaker as she listened to Kaleb's words. *"I've been going over this thing between us from start to finish, including the day I saw you at Home Depot and . . . something doesn't add up for me. . . ."*

Her eyes squinted and she sat up straighter as she held the phone in her hand.

"Because, see, I love you and I know this energy . . . this chemistry, between us is real. To hell with age differences and crap. We got the stuff a lot of people search for their whole lives. . . ."

She smiled as she listened to the rest of his message. It was just the final piece to any questions in her mind nagging at her. Zaria knew she loved Kaleb. She even knew he loved her. And she knew that his proposal was all about love and not just about the baby.

Jumping up from the bed, she raked her fingers through her hair and pulled the T-shirt down over her hips before she padded out of the bedroom. She paused and pulled her T-shirt down over her thighs as the crowd of people all gathered in the living room and kitchen went completely quiet and turned to eye her.

"Not again," one of the brothers drawled.

Zaria was sure she looked like a deer caught in the headlights. "Good morning, everyone," she said, not recognizing half the people.

Kaleb stepped through the crowd and came up to press a kiss to her temple. "We'll be right back," he said with a big grin before turning to push Zaria back into the bedroom.

"Is that your whole family, Kaleb?" she asked, her voice incredulous.

Kaleb nodded. "Someone at the hospital saw me there and called my moms and she called me all upset and wondering what happened . . . and I kinda gave them the good news about the baby and the engagement."

Zaria walked up to him and wrapped her arms around his waist. "And they all just climbed into vehicles and came over?" she asked, placing kisses along his neck and inhaling his scent.

"And made breakfast," Kaleb added with a chuckle as he wrapped his arms around her as well.

Zaria leaned back to look up at him. "And you think I can handle all them out there?" she asked.

"You are just the woman to do it," he assured her.

Zaria grunted in disbelief. "My doctor's appointment is today," she told him.

"Good, because I want to know when we get the all-clears for a real makeup session," he said.

Zaria laughed, but then nodded. "You know what . . . I agree."

Kaleb swatted her buttocks. "That's my girl."

They moved apart as Zaria pulled on her jeans with the T-shirt.

"You're coming to my brother's wedding today, right?"

Zaria nodded. "If you want me to."

"I want you to. You and the girls."

Zaria felt like she really could have her happily-ever-after.

"You ready to do this?" he asked.

Zaria nodded and slipped her hand into his. "Let's do this."

Kaleb took a sip from his glass of champagne as he watched Zaria from across the room. The female members of the Strong family were gathered at one of the linen covered tables talking and laughing. With Zaria. That was important to him because family was everything to him and he wanted Zaria, his future bride and mother of his unborn child, to feel comfortable around them. They were a huge lot and it could be overwhelming at first.

"And then there was one bachelor left."

Kaleb turned as his father stepped up to stand beside him. "Yesterday I was feeling like I lost her forever and today I have her and a new baby on the way," he said, unable to stop the grin from spreading across his handsome face.

"The way I see you watching her reminds me of how your mother had my nose wide open when we first—"

Kaleb cleared his throat loudly. "I feel a TMI coming," he drawled, shaking his head in refusal.

Kael chuckled. "I was going to say when we first got married."

"Oh. Okay."

Kael reached up and affectionately patted and then rubbed the back of his son's head. "I'm proud of my boys," he said, his voice warm.

"Thanks, Pop," he said, remembering that the

head pat and rub was his dad's version of a hug when they were coming up.

"Now if I can just do something about that daughter of mine," he said, his grip on Kaleb's head tightening.

Kaleb frowned. Deeply. "A'ight, Pops," he complained shaking off his father's strong grasp as he followed his father's line of vision locked and loaded on Kaitlyn as she danced without a care in the world.

"She's going to Paris, ain't she?" Kaleb asked, thinking his sister was having way too much fun to have *not* gotten her way.

"You know it," he admitted.

Kaleb just shook his head and laughed, as he watched Garcelle hand the baby to Zaria to coo and coddle. *Soon that will be our child in her arms,* he thought, loving the idea of that.

His father disappeared from his side and reappeared just moments later. Kael nudged him, his eyes locked across the tent on his wife. "Watch this, young buck. Watch and learn," he said.

Suddenly the first strains of the soulful bassline of the upbeat *Lovely Day* by Bill Withers began to play and Kaleb watched as his mother suddenly sat up straight in her chair and began frantically looking around the entire tent and its close to a hundred inhabitants until she finally laid eyes on her father.

Kaleb looked back and forth between his parents as they shared a long look and a wiggle of their eyebrows. His father began to move his shoulders, work his feet and snap his fingers as he bit his bottom lip.

His mother jumped to her feet and flung her head back as she began to dance across the crowded dance floor toward her husband as she snapped her fingers and grooved as well.

"That's our song right there. Watch and learn young'un," Kael said loudly over his shoulder, as he dipped his shoulders and began dancing away with a two-step that was soulful. "Watch. And. Learn. Hey!"

Kaleb smiled and laughed as he watched his parents eye each other until Kael grabbed his wife around her waist and twirled her in the middle of the dance floor. Everyone on the dance floor began to back away and surround them, leaving Kael and Lisha dancing together with smiles on their faces, like no one else existed or mattered as they sang the song to each other.

"Then I look at you and the world's alright with me . . ."

Kaleb sought Zaria's eyes and his heart swelled to see her dancing toward him on her four-inch heels. Laughing and clapping, he licked his bottom lip and moved toward his future bride with a soulful two-step. As soon as he neared her he pulled her body close and they rocked together like they were trying to win a *Soul Train* dance contest.

"Alright now," Zaria said with a smile when Kaleb circled her and held her close from behind. With their bodies pressed close together, they rocked together to the floor and brought it up.

Looking beautiful in her cocktail length lace and satin dress, Jade pulled Kaeden onto the floor with two hands. Bianca led Kahron onto the dance floor, followed by Garcelle and a reluctant Kade.

All of the reception goers watched the entire Strong clan partying and having a good time in the middle of the dance floor. There was no doubting the love they had for one another and their significant others.

EPILOGUE

Six months later

"Am I crazy to be getting married? Look at me, I'm as big as a double wide trailer," Zaria asked, studying her reflection in the full-length mirror. "It's hot as—"

"Ma, we're in church," Meena said from behind her with urgency.

Zaria clamped her gloss covered lips together and used a wedding program to fan herself. "Just roll me down the aisle and tell Kaleb to put his foot out like a kickstand to stop me at the altar," she said dryly.

Neema and Meena stepped up on either side of her, looking really pretty in their rose petal strapless chiffon dresses with knee-length skirts and thin rhinestone headbands in their updos. "Ma, you look beautiful," they said in unison.

Zaria shrugged as she took in the beautiful chiffon one shoulder wedding dress she wore with an elaborate design of oversized rosettes on the shoulder. The empire waist emphasized and framed her full breasts before flowing into a long and elegant skirt that showed nothing but the tips of her painted toes. Her make-up was flawless. Her hair was in an elegant updo with a floral rhinestone headband.

"I do look pretty good," she admitted begrudgingly, her hands coming up to cup her swollen abdomen.

"And everything is fine," Neema added, pressing her bouquet into her hands. "It's going to be the perfect wedding."

Zaria nodded, giving both her girls an air kiss before she twisted her bouquet in her hands. It was the final piece to her happily-ever-after. She had moved into Kaleb's home and turned it into the showcase it deserved to be. She'd even taken over the running of the dairy store and found the nesting traits of her pregnancy worked well for organizing the store and maintaining the records—with Kaeden's help. Her girls had graduated with their associates degrees and both transferred to the College of Charleston to get their four year degrees. They even had part-time jobs and moved into the house with plans to take over the mortgage once they graduated.

She had a relatively easy pregnancy for her age and things with Kaleb were better than she hoped. *Life is good. Enjoy it.*

Determined to do just that, Zaria smiled and turned away from the pity party she was having with herself in the mirror. There was a brief knock at the door before it opened. Zaria turned to see Lisha, Garcelle, Jade, Bianca and Kaitlyn all walk in looking beautiful in an array of summer sundresses.

"We just wanted to check on you before the ceremony," Lisha said, coming over to hug Zaria close. "You look beautiful."

"Thank you," she said, loving that the women had all made her and her daughters feel welcomed into the family. She worried that because she was closer to Lisha's age than her soon to be sisters-in-law that they would judge her—but they hadn't. From the moment Zaria first met them the morning they all crowded into Kaleb's house, Zaria's wit and fun nature had caused them all to gel. Thankfully.

"I'm so glad you two realized that you had been on the same page the whole time," Lisha whispered to her with a quick peck to her cheek.

Zaria leaned back and laughed.

"Alrighty, we got a wedding so let's get to our seats, ladies," Lisha said, nudging her daughters out the door even as they all wished Zaria well and gave her tips for remaining calm.

Soon the wedding planner led Zaria and the twins out of the back room and into the foyer. As she listened to the music playing softly, each of her daughters rubbed her belly and squeezed her hand before they stepped through the archway and walked down the white covered aisle of Holtsville Baptist Church.

She had just stepped in the doorway herself, as the wedding planner arranged her dress behind her, when she felt the first twinge of discomfort. Everyone in the church rose and turned to look at her as she began her march down the aisle. She rested her eyes on Kaleb, looking tall and handsome in his hand tailored lightweight suit that was the color of dark sand and perfect for their small summer wedding.

Another twinge radiated and Zaria frowned a little at the increased intensity. Pressing a smile to her face, she took a few more measured steps down the aisle before a spasm hit her that made her nearly snap the stem of her bouquet in half. *Oh no . . .*

Seeing the look of concern on the faces of their family and close friends, she gave them a tight smile before looking down the remainder of the aisle at Kaleb.

"I love you," Kaleb mouthed.

Zaria's heart tugged and she gave him a wink. "I love you too" she mouthed back.

Not now, little one. Mama's trying to marry Daddy and I absolutely refuse to plan another wedding . . .

By the time Zaria reached Kaleb at the altar there were tiny beads of sweat across her brow and the top of her nose. Kaleb eyed her oddly and then with concern. She slid her hand into his as they faced the minister, who peered at her over the rim of wire framed spectacles.

A spasm hit her and she squeezed his hand tighter as her eyes widened. "Ow!" Kaleb frowned and his eyes widened as the bones of his fingers pressed together. His knees dipped. "What the—"

The minister stopped, and closed his bible with his finger, as he eyed them.

Zaria felt the murmurs of the people behind them. "I'm in labor," she whispered as she closed her eyes.

"Huh?" Kaleb, the minister, and the twins asked in unison, leaning in toward her.

"The baby's coming," she admitted.

Kaleb wrapped his arms around her waist. "Alright, baby. Let's get to the hospital."

"Awesome," the twins said in unison.

The minister cleared his throat. "Ladies and gentlemen, the wedding has to be postponed—"

Zaria held up her hand. "Oh no, we are going to do this right now, Rev," she insisted. "I'm not going anywhere until we've stuck a fork in this wedding hoopla."

Zaria heard the footsteps of their family and friends coming from the pews to surround them. The sudden heat of their bodies irked her a bit. The clamor of the voices protesting with her really kicked her agitation up a notch.

"Baby, we have to get to the hospital," Kaleb whispered in her ear as he attempted to guide her out of the church.

Zaria gave herself a three count before she opened her eyes and looked at the Reverend. "Just finish," she insisted, giving him a stern look. "My water hasn't broken. It's just labor pains. It's not the end of the world people. The time it's taking y'all to complain and try to change my mind, we could have been done and on the way to the hospital."

The minister shifted his eyes to Kaleb. He nodded, tightening his grip around her body.

"Remember to breathe through your mouth, baby," Kaleb whispered to her as the minister began the ceremony.

Zaria nodded and pursed her lips through

another contraction. She barely focused on the minister's words of love and commitment as she concentrated on her breathing.

"Rev, let's just cut to the chase," Kaleb said, his concern for Zaria evident.

"Right," he said with a nod.

Zaria reached her free hand out toward her daughters and they both clutched it tightly.

"Do you, Kaleb, with all the love, commitment, patience, forgiveness, and devotion needed for a lasting union, take Zaria to be your lawfully wedded wife?"

"I do. I do," he promised, before pressing a kiss to her damp brow.

Zaria clenched his hand again at another contraction. She smiled a little when she felt his hand stiffen to keep her from crushing his fingers. "You ready this time, huh?" she asked.

"You know it," Kaleb assured her.

The crowd around them laughed lightly.

"And do you, Zaria, with all the love, commitment, patience, forgiveness, and devotion needed for a lasting union, take Kaleb to be your lawfully wedded husband?" the minister asked, looking at her over his spectacles.

Zaria nodded, lifting her head to look at Kaleb with a soft smile. "I do," she told him with earnest. "I really do."

The crowd sighed.

Kaleb's eyes searched hers as he gave her a bit of smile in return.

"Now by the power vested in me by the state of South Carolina and under the spiritual governance of God, I hereby declare these two beings into one legal and spiritual union only to be separated upon death. You may kiss your bride . . . and get her to the hospital."

Kaleb and Zaria kissed as the crowd applauded and laughed.

Another contraction hit her and Zaria let her legs go out from underneath her.

Kaleb swung her into his arms as the crowd opened to allow him to stride up the aisle. Their limo driver looked surprised by their sudden appearance and rushed to open the door.

"Get us to Colleton Memorial," Kaleb demanded as he eased Zaria onto the seat and then climbed in behind her.

"Yes sir," he said, racing across the car to climb into the driver's seat.

Zaria was glad when Kaleb leaned her back against him. "We're having a baby," she said softly.

Kaleb laughed.

There was a knock at the window just as the limo pulled off. Kaleb looked at the twins running beside the limo. "Stop," he ordered the driver.

They opened the door and carefully climbed in.

Zaria was glad for their presence. "And baby makes five," she said, looking over at them.

"Awesome," they said in unison.

The foursome laughed as the limo sped away from the church.

It wasn't until Kaleb left the delivery room, still dressed in his scrubs, that he realized that their entire wedding had come to the hospital. He was expecting to see just the twins but his handsome face filled with surprise as nearly thirty people rose to their feet in the small waiting room.

"Zaria's fine. It's a boy. Our son. Kasi Dean Strong," he said, feeling like he was on a natural high.

Everyone rushed forward to embrace and congratulate him.

His step-daughters. His parents. His brothers. His sister. His sisters-in-law. Niece. Nephews. Cousins. Friends. He felt surrounded by love and didn't bother to stop the huge smile that spread across his face in that moment because he realized that everything he hoped and dreamed for had come to fruition.

Dear Readers,

Thanks again for the love and support and desire you have shown for the Strong family series. I hope you have come to care for these characters as I have. Zaria and Kaleb had to fight and face so many obstacles outside of them and inside of them before they gave in to a love that they both needed like rain for a drought and food for the hungry. Love makes all things possible, and these two soon found that chemistry brought them together but love will keep them together. And that's what romance is all about, right?

Next up, the baby sister of the clan. She's lovable and fun and spoiled beyond belief by her father and all of her brothers. It's going to take a special man to tame this wild woman, and I have someone just right in mind—Quinton "Quint" Wells. I haven't selected a fiery title yet, but please stay tuned for more details on this final tale of love and romance for the Strong family clan.

Here's wishing you lots of real love and real romance to last a really long time.

Best,

Niobia

About the Author

Niobia Bryant is the acclaimed and bestselling author of more than twenty works of fiction in multiple genres. She writes both romance fiction and commercial mainstream fiction as Niobia Bryant. As Meesha Mink, she's the coauthor of the popular and bestselling Hoodwives series (*Desperate Hoodwives, Shameless Hoodwives,* and *The Hood Life*) and kicked off her own solo Real Wifeys trilogy with *Real Wifeys: On the Grind.* The Newark, New Jersey, native currently lives in South Carolina where she writes full-time. She is busy at work on her next piece of bestselling fiction.

Connect with Niobia:

Web site: www.NIOBIABRYANT.com
E-mail: niobia_bryant@yahoo.com
Twitter: /InfiniteInk
Facebook: Niobia Bryant-Meesha Mink (Announcement Page)
Facebook: /InfiniteInk (Personal Page)
Myspace: /niobiawrites
Shelfari: /Unlimited_Ink
GoodReads: InfiniteInk
Yahoo Group: /Niobia_Bryant_News

PROLOGUE

It's amazing how pain—that deep, searing, emotionally based heartache—can eventually lead to feeling completely numb. The line between the two is way thinner and flimsier than the one floating between love and hate. The jacked-up part was, Nylah Lovely knew about each line very well, and in that moment, she drifted across both.

Bzzz . . . bzzz . . . bzzz . . .

Her body was stiff with shock, afraid to move, afraid to do anything to intensify the pain that felt as if she had been shot by a bullet and not shocked by the truth. And so nothing but her pain-filled eyes shifted from the computer to take in the vibrating cell phone on the edge of her desk.

"Do you want me to get it?"

Her eyes shifted to the concerned face of her best friend, Tashi Oyoni. "No. It's either Byron with more lies or the press with more questions and speculations," she said softly, barely above a whisper before she sighed as she forced her body to lean back against the leather sofa of her best friend's home. "I don't have it in me for either."

Falling in love and getting married was risky no matter what the circumstances. Everyone took a chance on placing their heart into someone else's hands and could only hope not to have it crushed within their grasp. Love under the spotlight was even more tenuous. It felt like groupies, bloggers, and the entertainment news media were drooling, waiting to hear about one of the mighty falling. Like her husband, multiplatinum R & B star Byron Bilton.

Their entire relationship had been chronicled, from the first spotting of them trying to have a low-key dinner at a tucked-away restaurant to their two-year relationship and subsequent fairytale marriage at a castle—and everything in between. They knew her name, they took her picture, but truly they forgot about the person out of the limelight—the noncelebrity—just trying to be happy in her relationship, just trying to make it work, just trying to enjoy being in love. That person became a casualty of something they simply considered news.

They cared nothing about her shame, her pain, her heartbreak. Her embarrassment. And yes, yes, she was woman enough to admit that having his infidelity exposed to the world before she even knew and could process it made the pain all the more worse. All the more haunting. All the more difficult to forgive . . . or forget.

What woman—what person at all—would want to discover that their husband had cheated via some blog post showing the crappy cell phone video of him, his privates, and some faceless woman?

Bzzz . . . Bzzz . . . Bzzz . . .

Tashi looked down at the BlackBerry. "It's Byron again. Do you want me to answer it?"

Love said nothing. She had nothing to say.

She had nothing to say to him. She had so much to say to him.

Another line to swing back and forth over.

"Byron, hold on, Love's right here."

Her eyes widened as she looked up at Tashi setting the cell phone on the table in front of her.

"Love," he said, his deep voice echoing.

"You put him on speaker?" Love mouthed, her face incredulous.

Tashi immediately looked apologetic. "I'm sorry," she mouthed back, before biting her bottom lip.

"Love, I know you don't believe that bullshit."

Love's eyes shifted again to take in the photo. "I know that I am looking at a picture of your privates snuggled deeply in a woman's mouth . . . in our condo . . . on our couch . . . during the weekend I went home to Holtsville," she said, her voice hollow.

"Love—"

"I know that we were supposed to celebrate

our anniversary in another week. Celebrate *our* love. *Our* devotion." She laughed bitterly. "But you never were ready for this. You are not the one for me. You are not going to be my husband. Or my lover. Or in my life anymore. *That* I know."

"Love—"

"And I know that you need to give me fifty feet, because I didn't need to find out in a fucking blog that the man I love ain't shit," she finished in a harsh whisper, tears filling her eyes before she closed them as a sharp and piercing pain radiated across her chest.

One solitary tear filled with the weight of her pain raced down her cheek.

"I love you—"

Love laughed bitterly before she picked up her BlackBerry and threw it away from her. It hit the mirror over the brick fireplace, shattering the glass.

"Oh, Love." Tashi sighed, coming around the table to wrap her arms around her shoulders and hug her up in some sistah-friend love that she needed.

The act of friendship and support shook her to her core and the dam broke from the act of compassion. The tears raced down her cheeks like an endless relay race to soak Tashi's cinnamon brown shoulder.

"Girl, what are you going to do?" her friend asked as she patted her back like a mother belching a newborn.

The question made Love weary deep in her soul. Everything about her life and the path she was on—with love and marriage and family—was just shattered into a billion pieces and blown away by imaginary winds never to be reclaimed. Her life with Byron was over. It was way more than she wanted to tackle at the moment.

Chapter 1

"Summer Lady"—Santana

Three Years Later
May

"If my lover could be the summer sun, I would lay naked beneath him, exposed and waiting for him to reach out to kiss and caress my skin as his heat would fill my body and his light would elevate my moods," Love said in a husky voice with just a tinge of her South Carolina accent slipping through as she stretched her long and slender limbs up as if she could touch the clear blue skies from where she stood on the rooftop of her brownstone. "If only my lover could be the summer sun, I would have no regrets and our love would last a lifetime. I would even share his brilliance with millions as long as he stayed available for me upon request."

She fought the urge to slip her silk robe from her body and truly let the sun bronze her already cinnamon brown complexion. Even though she owned the two-story brownstone and, thus, exclusive rights to its spacious rooftop, she had no desire to give her neighbors a peep show. Instead she wrapped her arms around her body and looked out at the city landscape as the sun rose in the sky. Harlem.

Once the mecca for African-American art and culture, the city was now known for more than just its historic Renaissance.

Love flew to its warmth and character in the months following the end of her marriage to Byron. It was the place that embraced a wounded sistah needing to flee the flashing lights of the paparazzi as she tried to recover from the hurt and embarrassment from where she lived on the Upper East Side. Harlem's warmth nurtured her. The sense of community embraced her. The success of its revitalization revived her. The beauty of the brownstones intrigued her. The history healed her.

Duke. Langston. Billie. Ella.

And now Love.

There was nothing better than sitting on the rooftop just as the sun began to rise and writing about her day in her leather-bound journal. Knowing she was in the city that nurtured art and culture, and maybe even sitting on the same roof as a famous Renaissance writer, made her feel more connected to her words and their composition.

She smiled softly as she picked up her sweating glass of peach tea from the ledge of the roof.

Only the hint of summer was in the air, but she could feel it coming. And she couldn't wait. Love had a jones for the summer season. There was a whole new life and vibrancy to Harlem during the summer months. Everything got kicked up a notch.

The entertaining on rooftops.

The summer festivals in the park.

The sounds of music of many genres mingling in the air.

Gospel brunches.

Lovers strolling down the tree-lined streets at a pace that could be considered lazy by those who just didn't understand how to relax and enjoy the moment.

It was only May, but summer was almost home in Harlem.

She smoothed the edges of her shoulder-length hair pulled up into a loose chignon and took a deep sip of her home-brewed peach tea before she tilted her head back and allowed the rays to kiss her neck and the soft brown skin exposed in the vee of her robe. She hated to leave it, but other duties called for the day.

With one last soft release of air, Love turned and padded barefoot across the brick-paved rooftop to the large black metal door. "If my lover could be the summer sun," Love said, with one last look at the sun over her shoulder before she walked through the door, down the short flight of stairs, and across the hardwood floor of the hall to her brownstone's third floor.

She loved her brownstone. It was a mix of the

building's original 1900s architecture, with moldings, a fireplace, and hardwood floors, and plenty of contemporary upgrades and modern design.

The entire building could fit inside the living room of the apartment she had shared with Byron on the Upper East Side, but this felt more like home than any of the three residences she walked away from. Everything about the warm décor with small hints of fuchsia was her. She never regretted her decision two years ago to move to the Hamilton Heights section of Harlem.

It was a different pace—one that she desperately needed.

Trying to heal her broken heart under the lights of paparazzi and bloggers had nearly broken her. She felt like she didn't want to leave the house. She got tired of the hoopla. She got frustrated with the fame.

True, her event-planning and design company, Lovely Events, had a celebrity client list filled with athletes, musicians, and actors, but she had found the balance between promoting them and their events while staying in their shadow.

Unlike celebrities' wives before her who had been done wrong, she had no comment to release, no publicist to tell her side, no wish to grace the pages of *Essence, Vibe,* or *Vanity Fair* to sing her sad song. She had a life to rebuild and a thriving business as an event planner on which to place her focus.

Like the wedding she was planning today.

Although she planned out every minute detail to the likes of her clients—and to ensure that her signature taste level was achieved—there still was a lot to do.

She rushed across the living room and down the short hall to her master bedroom. Her cell phone was vibrating on the center of her unmade all-white bed. She never took it or her house phone onto the roof. She considered that her time to unwind and get her thoughts clear for the day ahead or to sit under the stars and reflect on the day behind her.

Slipping out of her robe, she grabbed up her cell just long enough to answer the call and put it on speakerphone before sitting on her ebony dresser. "Hey, Tashi," she said, reaching into the long drawer to remove undergarments. She selected a deep purple sheer bra and matching thong.

"You haven't changed your mind about letting me slip into the wedding today?"

Love rolled her eyes and smiled as she sprayed her favorite perfume, Lovely by Sarah Jessica Parker, all over her body. "Tashi, you know I am not letting you crash these people's wedding. You can forget about it."

"That's what friends are for," Tashi sang through the line, very off-key.

"I offered to let you work for me and you turned me down," Love said, walking across the room to her closet—the one complaint of the apartment. It was more of a step-in than a walk-in.

"Work? It's Saturday! I did my forty hours for the man this week," she balked.

Love just laughed as she shook her head. "Talk to you later, Tashi," she said, grabbing a tailored black satin skirt and a top with sheer blouson sleeves.

"Guess I'll have a spa day or something . . . but you . . . um, you take care. I know how weddings get to you."

Love paused in pulling the skirt up over her hips to lock eyes with her reflection in the mirror hanging on the inside of the door. Tashi was her best friend and she had been there through all the mess and stress of Byron's betrayal. "I'm good . . . but thanks, girl," she said, before moving over to pick up her cell. "I'll call you later."

She ended the call and forced herself not to think about the past as she finished getting dressed.

"Girl, you were born to fulfill dreams."

"I'm glad we were able to bring your vision to life." Love smiled warmly as she eyed the look of pleasure on the bride and groom's faces. She always could tell if she truly hit the mark with her event planning and design by the look on a client's face. *Another satisfied customer,* Love thought as she rubbed her slender hands together in front of her.

When she moved from small-town Holtsville, South Carolina, to New York to attend college, her plan was to take the city by storm. She loved her down-home raising, but she always felt that there was so much more of the world to explore out of the small-town limits. Ever since she could remember, she knew she was headed up north first chance she got. College was her way out.

And it was the best four years of her life, living

on campus, studying, exploring the city, and planning the small events of friends, on-campus clubs, and some of the faculty. Once she graduated, she was filled with big dreams, a huge sense of style, and a head for business. She eventually set up her own event-planning business on the side, and within a few years, her business began to grow through word of mouth and press for her uniquely planned events.

But then she met Byron at one of her charity events and everything changed. Everything. Love happened. Big-time. His jet-set life and powerful friends became hers as well. Two years later they wed. Their contacts helped her expand her brand and her business. She never thought she would go from being a small-town girl just making it in NYC to being both the wife of an R & B superstar and one of the premiere event planners in New York, catering to celebrities, athletes, and the wealthy elite.

In their marriage, her career had thrived; unfortunately, her heart hadn't fared that well.

Love pushed away any sad thoughts of love lost—or rather crushed—as she guided the couple out of the elaborately decorated ballroom to an outer room designed with subtle hints of their chocolate and ivory wedding colors, a bottle of their favorite Veuve Clicquot champagne, and light appetizers.

"Just relax and enjoy the moment as we finish up the cocktail hour and then get all of your guests seated," Love told them, her soft voice very calming and relaxing. "We should be ready to announce you in about ten to fifteen minutes, and again, congratulations—here's to the rest of your lives together."

With one final reassuring smile, Love slid her slender figure out the door just as the multimillionaire football quarterback and his new bride shared a deep kiss. As soon as the door closed, her smile faded just a bit. It wasn't that she wasn't happy for her clients; she just wasn't disillusioned about how long the happiness would last.

Been there. Done that.

As an event planner, it was Love's job to plot, plan, and execute every detail for charity events, awards galas, dinner parties, and red-carpet events . . . but weddings were the worst for her since her divorce a few years back. Everyone focused on the wedding and not many gave a bootie-toot about the marriage. And with him being a high-profile athlete, the battle was going to be even tougher for them with the world's focus on celebrity and fame.

But her job was to focus on the wedding day, not warn them about how tenuous love could be under the spotlight.

Love paused at the entrance to the ballroom and placed a hand to her chest as she took a moment to get herself together. This day—and any day she was at an event for a client—wasn't about her. Her issues. Her problems. Her drama.

She let nothing affect her professionalism.

Love always stayed cool, calm, and totally collected.

Always.

After a quick walk-through of the cocktail hour

in the spacious library, Love quickly checked in with her staff to ensure they were following her strict instructions. She took a moment to look out the large floor-to-ceiling windows of the semicircle foyer. It was a beautiful day out, but she was glad they opted against any outdoor activities. That would've meant more work and more challenges for her. More planning. More—

Love did a double take, locking her wide expressive eyes on the tall and slender man climbing out of the back of a huge SUV with blacked-out windows. Her heart pounded as he turned, but she didn't need to see his face or his two burly bodyguards to know it was her ex-husband. They began to walk up the steps together toward the front door.

"Shit," she swore.

Flustered, she made an un-Love move and clumsily backed away from the window before she turned and fled into the guest bathroom off the foyer. She pressed the button on her wireless headset. "Faryn, um . . . is . . . is . . . my ex-husband on the guest list for the reception? I know he wasn't at the wedding. Was he?" she asked, nearly slipping on a wet spot in four-inch vintage Gucci heels.

"No, Ms. Lovely. Let me check something. One sec."

Love paced.

"It had to happen, Love," she advised herself. "You couldn't avoid him forever."

Love hadn't been alone with her ex since the day the story broke about his cheating. She stayed with Tashi until he moved out of their penthouse, and anytime after that, they were accompanied by their lawyers hammering out their divorce. He was always busy touring or in the studio, and she always made sure to steer clear of any red-carpet events, parties, or premieres that she knew he would attend.

"Shit," she swore again, hating the unexpected. The unplanned. The sudden pothole in the road.

The press would have a week or two worth of speculations about the awkward meeting between Byron Bilton and his done-wrong ex-wife. Love *hated* to be in the press outside of mentions or blurbs about her events. She wanted her personal life to be . . . personal.

She turned on the gold faucets and lightly dampened a hand towel to moisten her neck and behind her ears. Now she wished Tashi were there with her. They met when she hired her as her personal assistant just a little over three years ago. After just four short months, Tashi moved on to a less stressful job, but their friendship had lasted. Her friend was the bold one with the quick wit and snappy comebacks for days. Tashi would know what to say. What to do.

Love licked the peach-tinted lip gloss on her full heart-shaped mouth before releasing a stream of air through pursed lips. There was the slightest tinge of warmth and color around her long slender neck and high cheekbones. She used her fingertips to smooth her shaped brows and the soft edges of her jet-black hair pulled up into a loose topknot. "Okay. All right. No biggie, Love," she said to her reflection, smoothing her satin skirt over her hips before she turned and left the restroom.

Beep.

"Go, Faryn," she instructed, closing the door behind her.

"Mr. Bilton was the last-minute plus one for one of the bride's guests . . . a Sasha Kilmore."

Love's steps faltered as she caught sight of her ex, and a woman she presumed to be Sasha, in the corner enjoying an impassioned embrace while his bodyguards pretended not to watch.

"Yes, I see that, Faryn," she dryly told her assistant. "Thanks."

Everyone turned at the sound of her voice, and all of the men's faces shaped with surprise.

Love locked eyes with her ex and then shifted them away. She took some pleasure in knowing the desire to slap the taste out of his mouth was gone. She hadn't known if she would ever get over that. "Excuse me," she said, polite and reserved.

Byron stepped away from his date. "Nylah, you're the event planner?" he asked, his voice just as husky and soulful as when he sang.

Byron was the only person to call her Nylah. The only one. All her family and friends back in Holtsville called her Love. The tradition continued once she went to school in New York. Back then, she thought it was endearing that he called her by her given name, but now she, ironically, realized that love—her name or the emotion—was no way in his vocabulary. She had loved and trusted this man with her heart, her soul, and her body. Hindsight is twenty-twenty.

She spotted the dark-skinned beauty trying to step forward, but both the guards blocked her path. Love rolled her eyes heavenward before she turned to walk down the hall.

"I don't want you to be uncomfortable, Nylah," Byron said from behind her.

Love paused, her back still to him.

"So I'll leave. Okay?"

Surprise and relief washed over her. She nodded. "Thank you," she said over her shoulder before hurrying forward, away from her past.